CW01210018

THE WINTER WIDOW'S DAUGHTER

VICTORIAN ROMANCE

DOLLY PRICE

PUREREAD.COM

CONTENTS

DEAR READER, GET READY FOR ANOTHER GREAT STORY...

A VICTORIAN ROMANCE

It's Christmas - a tearful mother leaves her beloved girl to fend for herself in an unforgiving Victorian world....

How will Tess survive?

Turn the page and let's begin

CHAPTER 1

PRESTON, LANCASHIRE

1845

When Teresa Woods was four years old, she heard about Christmas. It was a warm June Sunday, and the family, consisting of her father, mother, and herself, took their customary walk beyond St. Augustine's church toward the country, leaving the bad air of Preston behind for a few hours, for even on the day of rest, the smoke from the town's cotton mills did not clear from the industry of the last six and a half days. Preston in Lancashire was a busy, thriving place north of Manchester, and growing as opportunities for employment in textile mills caused many people from the surrounding country areas to make their way there to work.

Christmas was the farthest thing from the Woods' minds on this summer day when the birds sang, and the meadows were dotted with cheerful colour. People do not usually think of Christmas on summer days, but among the families out walking, they happened to meet Mrs. Boyce, a neighbour of middle age carrying a basket covered with a white cloth, who loved talking of her many ailments and of their suspected causes.

They were walking on a road with a pretty hedgerow, past a sprawling farm with hissing geese and clucking hens, and Teresa skipped ahead to pick wild blue cranesbill and yellow-eyed daisies which she gathered into the apron covering her pinafore. Mrs. Boyce was coming in the opposite direction.

"Good afternoon, Mrs. Boyce," was her father's greeting to the woman.

"And to you, Mr. Woods, and to you, Mrs. Woods." Mrs. Boyce nodded a greeting to Teresa's mother.

"How are you?" was Mrs. Woods' polite enquiry after she returned the greeting, ignoring the exasperated look from her husband, who wanted to get on and suspected that they would now be halted on the road for quite some time.

"Oh, I'm poorly, very poorly indeed!" Mrs. Boyce lamented, while Teresa crouched down and plucked purple corncockles and put them in her apron, taking little notice of the grown-ups talking among themselves.

Then began a litany of Mrs. Boyce's ailments, starting from pins and needles in two big toes, going onto her rheumatic knee, her delicate stomach, and flutterings in her chest, and ending by describing a funny sensation she got in her head from eating Christmas cake.

"Christmas cake? You still have some left?" Mrs. Woods asked her, surprised.

"Oh, very little now, for I couldn't eat it when I knew it was making me ill. I gave it away to, let's see. Mrs. Norris got a piece, and Mr. Kelly another, for he is thin you know, very thin, and the rest I offered to the vicarage maid, for the vicar has to entertain people, even the bishop. And the Stowes, when they came from Cumberland to see you, and I gave them some going away. But they're your relatives, aren't they? So, you know that, and have you heard from them at all of late?"

There was an uneasy pause. Jim and Belle Stowe were cousins of Mrs. Woods, who lived near Carlisle, and they had visited Preston to try to get them interested in one of Jim's schemes, to buy a share in some mining venture in Wales, promising a great return. But the Woodses knew Jim and Belle for the schemers they were and had refused. They could not afford to part with even the one pound asked, in any case.

"I gave them a pound, but I heard nothing at all. If you are writing to them, could you ask? I suppose you made the venture, too!"

"Em, no, we did not." Mr. Woods said.

"No? But it looked so promising! Oh well, never mind. I'm sure I shall hear something in time. I was speaking of the Christmas cake, and I do try to see what it is in it that doesn't suit me, that takes me away to the fairies in my poor head. I feel like I'm floatin' in th'air, up in the clouds like, and angels all about me, and I'm to enter Glory. Not that I'd mind tha', after all the troubles I've 'ad, ups and downs, ups and downs, I'm quite ready to go into Glory, but must wait for the Lord's timing. I hope it will not be too long now," she added, evidently hoping for a reassurance that the Lord would surely not call her just yet, which Mrs. Woods hurriedly supplied, murmuring that modern medicine could work marvels, and privately wondering why she was so willing to part with a precious twenty shillings when she expected to die before they returned to her with profit. Besides, she did not believe any of that religion talk, though Michael did.

It was the *fairies* and *angels* that got little Teresa's attention. She had dropped the corners of her apron and the flowers were now in a colourful heap tumbled on the road.

"Perhaps you put too much brandy in the Christmas cake," Mr. Woods said craftily.

"Oh, how wicked of you to say!" Mrs. Boyce frowned. "Brandy indeed! No, it's the nutmeg! Dr. Jones said it was the nutmeg. I must have forgot I put it in, for I had flutterings that day I did the Christmas baking, and then I must have put it in again. Then Gertie thought I hadn't put any in, stupid girl, and off she goes and puts in more, and when I looked at the bottle, it was only a quarter full. Well, I must be off home. I just took the last of it up to Mrs. Jenkins, and she gave me 'alf of a cream cheese in return. You shall have some when you get 'ome."

"That's very good, Mrs. Boyce," Mrs. Woods said as the woman bustled away.

"Papa, please help me put back the flowers!" Teresa held out her apron and lamented the heap of blooms at her feet. Mr. Woods obligingly began to gather them up and put them back into her held-out apron.

"The Stowes got at least one dupe in the village," Mr. Woods remarked as they began to walk on. "I wonder as 'ow many more were fooled."

"Michael, don't talk like that opposite the child."

"What's Chrissmas cake?" asked Teresa. "And why does eating it give you fairies in your 'ead? I'd like fairies in my 'ead. Can I get some?"

"Oh my, that child misses nothing. Hold out your apron properly, Tess, or you'll drop 'em all again, and this time you'll have to pick 'em up yourself," said her mother.

"Christmas cake is cake you eat at Christmas," her father replied. "And if you're very unlucky, for months afterwards when you visit your friends and relations."

"But what is Chrissmas?" Teresa asked.

Her father explained the festival to her, which she found intriguing. On Jesus' birthday, everybody ate Christmas cake. She became so interested in the subject that she let go her apron corners again and the flowers fell out, so she began to cry.

"They're all wilted now," said her mother. "Leave 'em be."

"I'll pick you a rose when we get 'ome." Her father said with gallantry. They had a pretty cottage, for her father was an overseer at Horrockses, the cotton mill, and he earned enough for the rent of their own cottage. Three rose bushes grew inside their gate. They were in full bloom.

Teresa reminded him of the rose when they returned, and he plucked one for her, a full-blown yellow, and one for her mother, which was red.

"One for Grandmama," Tess pleaded, and her father chose a white one. Mrs. Woods smiled with pleasure. Her mother and Michael did not always see eye-to-eye, but she would be delighted with the rose presented to her by her son-in-law.

They went inside. Grandmama had supper ready, cold ham, bread, butter, and tea, and some of the cream cheese that Mrs. Boyce had promised them. The roses were placed in a little glass vase and set in the middle of the table.

"Mama, will they wilt too?" Teresa asked sadly, her little fingers curling gently around her yellow petals.

"All flowers wilt, Tess."

"I don't want ‘em to die!" Tears began to roll down her cheeks.

"We can dry ‘em, Tessie child, and then you'll be able to keep ‘em always." Grandmama promised her. "I'll put them in a big book for you, if we can find one."

Her father offered his thick Roman Missal, with the hymns and prayers for all of the year in it, and Grandmama decided to use that.

Teresa forgot about the roses, but Christmas did not leave her mind for a week, when she wanted to know more and more about it, and was very crestfallen that it was not to be very soon, and that she had to wait for the leaves to fall and the weather to get cold. She forgot about it for a while. Then when the days shortened and the laneways filled with rain and dead leaves swirled about them, people began to talk of 'Christmas'. She remembered the cake, and she learned there was a lot more to Christmas than just cake. Mr. Pilkington's shop window was lit with bright lanterns and decorated with brightly-coloured papers and shiny ribbons, and people sang cheery carols on the street. Best of all, she heard talk of presents!

. . .

On Christmas morning she got up early. She saw the table laden with good things, and there was a sweet little rag doll with long yellow hair and a smiling face upon her own chair. She seized upon it and hugged it tight.

"Come on ter breakfast," urged her grandmother after she had been playing with the doll for an hour. She set a cup of warm milk on the table. "There, I've cut you a piece of Christmas cake for breakfast. Aren't you pleased?"

Teresa's brown eyes widened at the sight of the heavy fruit cake bordered with white icing and with its numerous ingredients all mixed together in it. She saw currants and cherries. She bit her lip. If she ate that cake, would she have fairies in her head and be on her way to Glory?

"Well, what's the matter wi' you? Don't you like cake, then?" her grandmother asked humourously.

"Oh, Ma, really, why did you give 'er cake for breakfast?" Mrs. Woods was banging the grate with a poker to get the flames going and making a tremendous racket.

"Now stop frettin' over the goose," said her mother. "There's only ourselves to eat it this year, with your poor father and Pete gone. As for cake for breakfast, why not? It's Christmas! Eat it up, Tessie love. Ah, there's Michael!"

Mr. Woods appeared, dressed in his best for Christmas Morning Mass. His hair was oiled, his moustache was waxed, and his collar was pristine. He wore his good suit and his shoes shone. He had a high hat upon his head.

"Why isn't Tess ready?"

"She's too young to go to church," said her mother.

"Not at all. She can sit quietly. Won't you sit quietly, little Princess?"

Teresa beamed, her mouth full of crumbly cake and a ring of white around it from the milk. She had never been to Mass before. She thought only men went to Mass, for her mother and grandmother did not go.

Her grandmother got her dressed very quickly, and soon she was attired in her Sunday coat and hat, and together father and daughter set off through the town hand in hand. She had never been in the church before, and she held his hand tightly when he led her halfway up the aisle. People were bustling in and taking their seats. She stared at very grand hats with feathers and birds' nests and big flowers in them. Music came from somewhere. Her father led her into a pew, and at his bidding, she knelt and joined her hands as he had taught her at home, though the only prayer she knew was to bless Papa, Mama, Grandma, and the Queen.

CHAPTER 2

CHURCH

The church was lit with more candles than she had ever seen in her life. They danced and twinkled. Amid much bell-ringing and chanting, the priests, deacons, and altar boys attired in white and red came from the sacristy and took their places around the gold-draped altar. The biggest altar boy stood inside the railing and shook a long silver flask about in all directions. He was holding it in one hand, and in his other hand was its long silver chain. The flask clinkety-clinked every time he shook it, and smoke came from it. It smelled strange, but very nice too. The Mass began but she could not understand any of it. People were very still and quiet when the priest raised the Sacred Host above him, and the bells rang out loud. It was suddenly very quiet in the church. People bowed their heads, and she did also.

"Stay 'ere, Tess." A short time later her father was following everybody up to the railing, but she was not to go.

Instead, she sat listening to the singing. But it puzzled Teresa that she could not see anybody singing anywhere. She stole a look around and still did not see anybody with their mouths open. Was this singing the doing of the Christmas cake? She shut her eyes the better to see fairies and angels floating about, and if possible, to join them, for it would be great fun to float about like them, but she saw nothing at all except the dark when her eyes were shut. She lifted her arms to see if she could float into the air, and waved her hands like a bird's wings, but she remained firmly on the seat. She heard smothered giggles behind her and looked about to see a boy laughing at her, his hands over his mouth. She put out her tongue at him and an old lady gave her a great big ferocious frown. Her father returned then and she quickly joined her hands together and pretended to pray as he was doing.

After Mass was over, they went to see the crib, and Papa gave her a penny to put in the poor box. As they came from the church, Teresa was dismayed to see the old lady approach.

"That child is too young to be brought to the church," she said with severity. "She does not know how to behave herself." And she went away.

"Some people have no Christmas spirit," said her father. "What did you get up to when I went up to Communion?"

"Nothing, Papa, nothing!" she protested, "But the boy behind me laughed at me for trying to fly."

"Trying to fly? What did you do, Princess?"

"Papa, I think I heard angels." she said solemnly. "Grandmama gave me Christmas cake for breakfast, and I heard singing, and I only put up my hands to try to float around the church. I tried and tried but I couldn't."

"What could have put that idea into your head, Princess?"

"Mrs. Boyce said that when you eat Christmas cake, you float around with fairies in your head." Teresa reminded him. "But maybe Grandmama didn't give me enough."

Mr. Woods had completely forgotten the walk of the summer before.

"The lady who comes to ask you if you heard anything," Tess reminded him, for poor Mrs. Boyce now had serious doubts about her investment, and popped her head in every now and then, enquiring. Teresa associated her always with Christmas cake, fairies, and angels in her head.

Now he remembered, laughed, and squeezed her hand.

"There were no angels singing that we could hear," he laughed. "No, my little Princess, the singing was coming from the choir loft. Someday I'll show you where the choir loft is. You know Miss Hughes? She sings in the choir. And Mr. Henderson."

"Oh," said the little girl, disappointed that only humans had made those angelic sounds, and very dull humans at that. Miss Hughes was not at all like an angel. She wore spectacles and an old brown bonnet and cloak. She walked with a stoop and was the farthest thing from an angel that she could imagine. Mr. Henderson was bald under his hat, though he sported long whiskers, and he carried a tattered old umbrella everywhere with him.

"Why didn't Mama come to Mass with us?" she asked then.

"She has to get the dinner, don't she?" her father replied. But it made him uneasy that already the little girl was asking awkward questions. Theirs was a mixed marriage. He was Roman Catholic; his wife was from a family to whom God was not important. Nobody had approved their union, not his family, nor hers. Her mother, and her father and brother Peter, now deceased, had accepted it in time, especially when they had moved in with the Woodses. His own kin lived in Essex and had never met his wife.

He and Elizabeth Fletcher had married in a rush of passion after knowing each other only six weeks, and soon after found out they had little in common. She thought him too serious and no fun, and he discovered a shallowness to her character and a flippancy about certain subjects he held dear. But the passion was still between them in the first few years. As time went on, the differences were becoming more annoying to each, while the passion began to slowly fade. It was difficult for one person to be a devout believer and live as such, and the other to hold such beliefs in contempt, especially when they had a child. Mrs. Woods had a little dishonesty Mr. Woods could not stand, and she could not bear his silent judgement when she regaled how much she had cheated the butcher that day. He ought to be pleased with her for being so canny about money!

Before they married, he had said that he wished their children to belong to his church. She agreed as long as he never expected her to go and never tried to convert her. Both kept this promise.

Teresa would probably be their only child. They had lost two before her to miscarriages. No other child had been conceived since her birth.

"But Mama never goes to church, Papa." Teresa reminded him.

Her father was silent. They had dealt with their sorrow in different ways, he and Elizabeth. He thought crosses a part of life and intensified his prayers; trying to love his wife more in what must be a greater sorrow to her than to him, and she saw and appreciated that, but did not share it.

At home in Friarsgate, Mama was indeed busy with pots, pans, and mixing bowls, and she was in no mood to talk. For her, Christmas was strictly a feast of the culture and had no religious connection. Teresa ran to retrieve her little doll which she had had to leave at home, and she carried it everywhere for the day.

"I love Christmas," she told her mother when she tucked her in that night, Bets, the new doll, clasped firmly to her heart. "Bets loves Christmas too, don't you, Bets? Why can't it be Christmas every day, Mama?"

"Because then we'd not enjoy it, would we, if we 'ad it every day of the year? Now close your eyes and go to sleep. Do you like your new doll?"

"Oh yes, Mama."

"Do you like her gown, then? Didn't the fairies sew it very nicely? See the little bow at the back, how good it's done! And the tiny embroidery at the collar? Isn't it pretty?"

"Oh yes, Mama! I love it. I love every bit of it."

"That's good then. Goodnight, dear."

"Say goodnight to Bets as well, Mama."

"Goodnight, Bets."

"I love Christmas," was the little girl's sleepy murmur. "How long before I have to wait before the next one?"

In the kitchen, the adults made tea.

"I suppose you'll be making more gowns for that doll, Elizabeth," her mother said with some cynicism. "You'll kill your eyes, you will. Wait until the days get long, at least."

Mrs. Woods was a very skilled seamstress. She made almost everything the family wore. She loved sewing, but her eyes often stung and hurt, and she could not work after daylight faded.

Mr. Woods had fallen asleep before the fire.

"Wake up, love, for your tea," she said, shaking him by the shoulder. He stirred and took the cup and saucer from her. He took a sip and began to cough. His face grew red with the violence of the cough as his wife took the shaking cup from him, laying it on the table, then bending her head over him, holding his handkerchief near his mouth. Her mother shook her head and stared at the fire. She didn't like these coughs of her son-in-law. It was bad, it was, and going on for some time now. It was the consumption that had taken Pete only last winter. It didn't bode well at all for him, or for her daughter and granddaughter, nor for herself, who had nothing put by.

The coughing ceased, he sat back in exhaustion, and Elizabeth rinsed the bloodied linen in a basin of cold water. There was an uneasy silence.

Asleep by now with Bets in her arms, Teresa did not hear him cough.

CHAPTER 3

PAPA

As the days grew longer and buds appeared on the trees, Teresa noticed that her father coughed a great deal. But too young to realise what it might mean, she played with her friends and was a happy child. She grew tall and healthy, and her mother was constantly letting down her hems to cover her bony knees as she shot up like a sapling in springtime.

When the daffodils blossomed and the birds sang in earnest, her father sat by the fire almost all day, pulling a blanket about himself to keep out the draughts. He coughed up blood. He did not go to work anymore, and men from Horrockses came to see him. Afterwards Tess became aware of a feeling of sadness in the house, though nothing was of course said, except for Grandmama remarking that they'd kept him on as long as they could, but now they'd have to let somebody else have his job.

They ate very plain food, and sometimes there was not enough, though her mother made a few potatoes go a long way and used up every little bit of food, There were foods that Tess never saw before, sheep's heads and backbones, and pig tails that her mother made soup from.

Mrs. Woods was the daughter of a master tailor. She used to attend to the female clients and was an expert dressmaker. Now her skills were called upon to provide for the family, but she had no clients and did not know how to begin. She sought piece work from an established dressmaking shop in Meadow Street, that of Miss Deuville's. She became tense and fussy as the work she brought home had to be spotless, and there was constant fear that they would be stained by an unnoticed spill on the table. The table had to be spotless.

Teresa found her mother rather cross at times, and it made her cry as they clashed.

Finally, her father had to stay in bed all the time, and Father Doyle came to see him every week. Teresa was not allowed to be present when he was there. She had to go outside. But one morning it was raining hard, and she, her mother, and her grandmother stayed in the other room in the cottage. That was when she heard her father sob out loud, *"What is to become of them? What will they do? They will be turned out of the house!"* She turned to her mother in distress. Mrs. Woods was weeping on her mother's shoulder. She put an arm about her little girl, and they huddled and cried together.

One day when she was sitting by Papa's bed, fiddling with the yellow ribbon on her long dark plait, he said, "Little Princess, do you know why you're a princess, then?"

She shook her head, surprised at his solemn question.

"Because your Father in Heaven, who is God, is a King. I'm going there soon. I will ask Him to look after you and Mama."

"And Grandmama," she reminded him.

"And Grandmama," he said. He said no more.

Her father died in May as the breeze blew pink and white showers of cherry petals around everywhere. Teresa had just turned five, and they moved from their little cottage on to a small room at the back of Mr. Collins' the grocers, in Hop Street. It was not a nice place. There was filth of all kinds in the yard outside, rotten fruit and vegetables which had to be swept up daily, and at the back was a stinking sewer running the length of the row of houses. Her mother cleaned the house and the yard in exchange for the room. It was too small for three, so Mrs. Fletcher had to enter the workhouse, and she never returned. After some time, Mrs. Woods told her that Grandma had died also.

"Is she in Heaven with Papa?" Her mother frowned.

"I don't want to hear any of that," she said shortly. "I won't have you believing stuff and nonsense."

Her husband was gone, and she could rear her daughter as she liked.

CHAPTER 4

SCHOOL

"You mun go to school now you're six," Mrs. Woods told Teresa.

But when Teresa told her little friends, she was distressed that Sophie and Mary were not to go to school. She did not want to go either.

"You mun go, I say so." Her mother said, her voice rising.

Teresa cried and stamped her foot, threw a tantrum, and shouted her protestations loudly. Her mother caught her and smacked the back of her legs with a wooden spoon.

"You'll go to school!" she cried angrily, over Teresa's howls. "I 'adn't a chance to learn anything, but you will learn! You're bright, I know you are. You'll learn to read and write and other things. You'll thank me for this one day!

Now stop bawling, or I'll beat you again. And remember the saying, *'them 'as 'as nowt is nowt.'* It means, if you 'ave nothing, you are nothing. Nothing! Do you 'ear me?"

Teresa lost the battle. She had to go to school whether she wanted to or not, and soon she and her mother were cordial again. Teresa knew that when her mother wanted her to do something, she had better do it. Mama was so often tired and cross, it made her unhappy too.

The little family moved again, this time to two rooms of their own, in a tenement building. It seemed luxurious compared to the stuffy, smelly room they had occupied before. It was not far from the school, so Tess could continue there.

Her mother made sure she was dressed nicely, was clean and tidy, and that she learned her lessons in the evening, sometimes being very strict about it. Teresa was a quick child, and she was very pleased about that, but if she came home with poor marks, she knew that she had to expect the wooden spoon. So, she worked hard, practising her reading and her letters, not allowing anything to distract her, not even when Sophie and Mary knocked at the window making signs for her to come and play with them. Soon, they stopped asking.

"You'll not be like me," her mother repeated to her time after time, her voice strong and determined. "Only able to write my name. You'll be educated and you'll get on in life.

Do you 'ear me?" she blinked her eyes painfully. She sewed long hours for Miss Deuville, and it hurt her eyes. "And you mun learn to sew, for as long as you can sew, and embroider, and especially if you can do fancy work, you can earn your bread, and easier than what your friends do. You won't be a factory girl. Now you sit there and practice your letters, I 'ave to go and take Miss Deuville 'er tablecloths."

Mrs. Woods made her way to the dressmakers in Meadow Street, a respectable area. Miss Deuville was very well known for two things. workmanship and quarrelsomeness. She had apprentices, and they were terrified of her. Any mistakes had to be ripped out and redone even if the girl had to stay late into the night and miss her supper, and if a girl made three mistakes in any work, she was dismissed. Miss Deuville had an eagle eye for even one uneven stitch among one hundred.

Her premises was the large downstairs part of a terraced house. Mrs. Woods knocked on the door and was allowed in by a servant who told her brusquely that her mistress was busy but to wait in here please. She entered a bright room where two girls sat at a table by the window, their heads bent over their work.

She stood waiting, the bundle of cloth in her arms, until Miss Deuville swept in with an impatient air. She indicated that she wished to see the work, and Mrs. Woods spread it on the table. The dressmaker's bony fingers flipped the tablecloths over.

"But what is this?" Miss Deuville was English but had affected a French name and accent. She had once been a ladies' maid. She was tall and gaunt with painted dark eyebrows and her hair was dyed black under her lace cap. "Why did you give them such large hems?"

"I gave them two inches, as you said, Miss Deuville," Mrs. Woods said, surprised.

"I did not say two inches! I said one inch and one half! My client will be angry. Take them away, unpick them all, and do it right. You will bring them to me tomorrow morning at nine."

"I remember you said two inches, Miss Deuville," Mrs. Woods protested. She looked desperately at the apprentices, but they pretended not to have heard anything. "And I asked you if you were sure? And you said yes, that your client wanted a generous hem."

Miss Deuville appeared to hesitate, but then her lips pursed in a thin line.

"You were distracted. I never said such a thing. If you wish to continue to work for me, you will redo these as I said, and pay more attention in the future." The conversation was over. She turned away and left through the door adjoining the other room.

Mrs. Woods had no choice but to sit up all night, and by the light of a tallow candle, she undid all of her work and then redid it. Teresa was fast asleep, her homework done, her books ready for school in the morning. She woke her at eight o'clock, gave her breakfast and sent her to school, and then trudged again to Miss Deuville's, and received only two shillings for all her work instead of the three that had been agreed upon. At home again, she collapsed onto her bed for a few hours, but woke again to shop and bake and cook dinner for Tess, which she ate at one o'clock. The afternoon was spent with more sewing, this time mending sheets for the inn. She was cross and tired when Tess came home from school and the girl did her homework in silence, wondering why her mother was in bad humour. She wished she could go out to play but did not dare ask.

Her mother, as if reading her thoughts, said, "I 'ave some sewing for you to do. You must learn button'ole stitch tonight."

Her heart sank, but she meekly obeyed.

Mrs. Woods had to work hard to keep her daughter in school, for it cost sixpence a week, and after that there were copy books and pencils. Sophie and Mary began work in the cotton mill. Teresa worked very hard, her face grew pale, and she felt that her mother was too hard on her. Other mothers were not like hers. She remembered her father and grandmother, and how happy she had been before they died, and wondered why everything had had to change, especially her mother. Sometimes she seemed like a harsh stranger, but other times, she was Mama, loving and cheerful. Tess never knew when to expect one or the other.

CHAPTER 5

CLARENCE

STAGTARN, CUMBERLAND

1846

Mrs. Bailey lifted her newborn son and smiled at the tiny round face and fair hair, very pleased. He was a healthy little fellow, and she congratulated herself heartily upon producing a male child, her first. She felt very proud of having such a sturdy infant, and he was worth the long labour, the horrendous pain, and the gigantic effort. She was exhausted, but what a great thing it was for your firstborn to be a son, especially as it was so desired not only by her, but by everybody in her own family! *Desired more than her husband ever suspected!*

There was a discreet knock on the door, and her husband, a large, red-haired rugged-faced man entered the room, bringing the scents of the farmyard with him. Not that she minded that, every smell meant money. His eight hundred sheep, nearly all of them Herdwick, all went about with a sum of money upon their woolly backs as far as she was concerned. And they belonged not to the Baileys. By rights, they belonged to her family, the Livingstones. But Ephraim did not know her thoughts.

"How are you, my dear?" he asked, bending his large frame awkwardly over the bed. She knew by his expression that he was very pleased indeed. "And is it -?"

He would surely love this boy more than the other, she thought.

"A boy! A boy! I have given you a son, a healthy son" she said proudly. "I wanted to tell you myself, so I asked Dr. Clarke not to tell you."

"When he said nothing at all, I thought it was a girl, and I didn't mind one way or th'other," he replied. He was easy-going, Ephraim Bailey. He was often referred to as a gentle giant, but his wife did not appreciate gentleness. She despised his easy nature, and she had married him only because she would be able to mould and manage him according to her and her family's plans and ambitions.

You fool, to not want a boy over a girl, she said silently. *Do you think Alexander will live to inherit the estate?*

Her son would inherit this large estate west of Carlisle, named Stagtarn, for her stepson Alexander, six years old, was a sickly boy. He would not live to adulthood, of that she was certain.

"I would like to call him Clarence Livingstone after my grandfather and my father," she said. She was sure he would grow up to be just like the Livingstone men, tough and uncompromising, with a head for business.

"Clarence Livingstone Bailey it is," he beamed.

Ephraim did not show any surprise at the choice of Livingstone as his son's second name, for that was the surname of his first wife Maria, Lydia's cousin, whom he had married when he was a lad, and she a lass, in 1825. They had been happy. She had died unexpectedly after nine years of marriage. Their only grief was that there had been no children.

His second wife, Alexandra, had died only two years before from scarlet fever. Her son Alexander had contracted it also, and he remained weak and ill after the severe infection that took his mother. He spent most of his time in the nursery, rarely leaving it. He was fading away there.

Lydia exulted that the way was open for her son to inherit Stagtarn Farm.

CHAPTER 6

STAGTARN HISTORY

Mrs. Bailey's father, Clarence, also known as 'Young Clary', came to visit the new baby, and they exulted together that the plan was going as they wished. It had been Lydia's grandfather's idea that she marry Ephraim, a man twice her age who had been married twice and widowed twice.

"I grew up in that house," Grandfather, known as 'Old Clary', Livingstone, was fond of saying when she was a child, and she would walk with him down the Long Road and see Stagtarn Hall loom out of the thickly wooded hillside. "I know every brick in it. A Georgian design, my own father went for, though putting it on top of a two hundred year old slate house gave the architect a headache. I remember it well, the arguments as to what walls to take away and what to leave. Eventually, the slate parts became barns, outhouses, and offices behind it, as you see it now, and the house itself fronting the road was all new. It cost a fortune, but by then the family had the mills. But wasn't it worth it? The finest house in the district, and a great prospect from the front. I wish it was ours still. It's wrong, wrong that it was taken from us. Now look at that stone wall, Lydia, in the field where you see the sheep grazing in front of the house. I built that with my own hands when I was sixteen years old. Look how it wends its way around and then winds all the way around the orchard. Isn't it a fine orchard? And the arboretum. My mother, your great-grandmother, planted those hollies when she was a young bride. Aren't they beautiful? She loved to see them covered in snow with the red berries showing through. They should be our holly trees, Lydia."

"I love the hollies, too, Grandfather. They're my favourite tree." She began to love everything about Stagtarn.

"Why don't we visit them?" Lydia said one time, curious to see the inside of the house.

"Oh no, we don't, not now. Not since the interloper."

From her earliest years, Lydia Livingstone had heard the sorry tale of how her family had lost their land, and how nobody of Livingstone blood now had any claim upon it. It was constantly lamented in the family.

The estate in Cumberland had belonged to the Livingstone family for hundreds of years, passing from generation to generation without any obstacle. When the industrial revolution began, the Livingstone fortune increased. They were an opportunistic family, and every generation was more successful, and even richer than the last, due to their buying textile mills in Leeds and Preston.

The disastrous loss of Stagtarn Hall and the lands had happened in very recent times. A great legal neglect had occurred one hundred years before. The legal arrangement to the male line expired and was never renewed. Therefore, as an only child, Maria Livingstone stood to inherit everything from her father John, whereas if the original arrangement had been in place, the closest male relative to John would have been heir to the house and land. That was his brother Clarence, the present-day 'Old Clary'.

At age twenty, Maria fell in love with the younger son of a neighbouring farmer who had nothing of his own. Her parents reluctantly approved the marriage. Maria became Mrs. Ephraim Bailey in 1825.

'Old Clary' left Cumberland for a time, as his bequest had been a thriving textile mill in Leeds, but he'd returned to build a house a mile from the family home, on a plot given to him by John. He settled his young family there, and in time, his son's family. It was by a small stream, so he named it Beckley House. From there he could see his brother's house, cream-coloured with its fourteen front windows. He only had eight. John had ten chambers more than he, as well as a billiard room, and even a terrace facing the flower garden. And all the land, sheep, pigs, and cattle. When he died, Maria and the interloper Bailey would get it all, and that is what happened. The Livingstone farm became the Bailey farm.

John's daughter Maria died suddenly nine years into her marriage and left no children. Stagtarn Hall now belonged solely to Mr. Ephraim Bailey, by law, and this was even more bitterly resented by the Livingstone family than when Maria was alive.

This was bad enough, but worse was to come! Only six months after the death of Maria, perhaps to alleviate his deep grief, Ephraim Bailey went away for a week and arrived home with a new wife. The Livingstone family were outraged at his haste. Alexandra, or Sandra, Grant was the new bride, and ten months later the Stagtarn lands had an heir, the sickly boy Alexander, who now languished upon the couch in the nursery. The heir to Stagtarn had not one drop of Livingstone blood. Their land was gone!

Old Clary, whose two granddaughters lived with him and were near to adulthood, saw his chance after the interloper's second wife Sandra died. Would Ephraim Bailey marry a third time? And would the sickly heir ever reach adulthood?

He decided to ask Dr. Clarke, who knew the family well, and who over a few drinks was likely to get a loose tongue. He was invited to dinner, and over port, the talk was brought around to the young heir of Stagtarn Hall and Estate.

"Will he live?" Old Clary had asked bluntly, with his son, Lydia's father, also present.

"The young master? There's not a chance he will reach his majority," Dr. Clarke had shaken his head mournfully. "No, he will not have many years, more's the pity."

Dr. Clarke had been a doctor for over fifty years. He must know what he was talking about. Old Clary began to scheme.

Lydia was the youngest, the prettiest, and most forward of his granddaughters, and he proposed the willing eighteen-year old to the lonely middle-aged man with the doomed, motherless child. For the second time in his life, Ephraim remarried swiftly after the death of his spouse, and now the third Mrs. Bailey, having given birth to a son within a year, was confident that her child would restore the lands back to their rightful ownership. The intention was that he would drop the name Bailey as an adult and revert to his second name as his surname.

Old Clary died a happy man soon after his namesake Clarence was born. Lydia's father would take up the torch now for the clan. Stagtarn Estate would be in Livingstone hands again soon.

CHAPTER 7

NEW DOCTOR

Baby Clarence Bailey thrived, became plump, toddled, and talked early, while in the other room, in the nursery, his brother Alexander lay on a day bed, weakened by the fever that had taken his mother and by the poor treatment he had received after his illness. Then Dr. Clarke became ill and retired, and a new doctor arrived. He came to see Alexander one day, as he was on the list of patients he had inherited from the old practitioner.

"How often does he go outside?" he asked his nurse, a middle-aged widow with wise, kind eyes. She was very pleased to see the new man. He looked energetic. Dr. Clarke evidently thought that Alexander was not worth the effort of trying to save. Nurse Wren had a different opinion. She had little education but a great deal of common sense and natural wisdom. She sensed that her mistress was not very interested in the recovery of her stepson, and she guessed why. She would have left this situation a long time ago, but she had grown very fond of her eldest charge.

"Mrs. Bailey does not permit 'im to ever go outside," she replied in a meaningful way.

"What? What about in summer?"

"She says that it's dangerous, the sun in summer and the cold in winter," Nurse Wren said forcefully.

Alexander was lying on the couch, lightly covered by a plaid blanket. He had been reading a book and it lay open to one side. He had a tall frame like his father, but he was very thin and pale. His blue eyes were enormous in his thin face, but Dr. Fellowes noted a quickness there as they followed his every move. The boy was paying attention to every word spoken.

"What are you reading, Master Alex?" Dr. Fellowes picked up the book. "Robinson Crusoe! My favourite book when I was your age!"

"I can't read very well. Mr. Naughton was reading it to me, but Nurse Wren is helping me now, sir."

"That was his tutor, Doctor, who was let go by the mistress as she felt he was too expensive," Nurse Wren said, with ill-disguised contempt. "But I don't read much myself, and it's quite difficult, but the pictures help him,

Doctor. I do wish he had someone to help him, as the Squire is always busy with the farm, and Mrs. Bailey with the house and her own child."

"What do you wish for, young man? Do you have any wishes?"

"I wish I could go on a big adventure!" Alexander said.

"And it is my job to try to make your wish come true," Dr Fellowes said brightly. "How long have you been sick now?"

"I don't know, sir."

"Four years," Nurse Wren said flatly.

"And you read a great deal, do you?"

"Yes, sir, it passes the time."

"Have you any friends calling to see you?"

The boy shook his head regretfully. He lowered his head.

"We are going to alter all that," the doctor said briskly. "We are new here in the district, and I have a boy your age. His name is Gerald. You must come and visit him. Bring the book with you, and perhaps you can make out all the big words between the two of you."

"Go out, sir? To your house?" The boy stirred himself on the couch and raised himself to a sitting position. His face lit up, his eyes shining with anticipation. Nurse Wren beamed.

"Yes, indeed yes. Next Saturday, about three o'clock."

On his way out, Dr. Fellowes met Mrs. Bailey in the large marbled hall.

“I have amended the course of treatment for the young Master,” he said briskly. “He will never get better languishing there as he does. He must go outside. Fresh air and exercise are vital for a recovering patient, and this is the healthiest place in all of England, I daresay. He never walks or runs as boys should, and his muscles will waste away if we do not remedy the situation.”

Mrs. Bailey was immediately on her guard.

“But he might get the grippe, Doctor. Or a lung inflammation.”

“He does not have to go out in the rain, Mrs. Bailey. If it is not raining Saturday, get him dressed and send him over to my house. My son Gerald and he are of an age, and Gerald has no friends as yet. The friendship will be good for both boys."

Mrs. Bailey frowned as she watched the doctor mount his horse and depart. She would send Alexander, rain or not, and if he should get inflammation of the lungs and die, it would only hasten the inevitable, but it disturbed her to see a hopeful doctor treating her stepson.

CHAPTER 8

AGRIPPINA

Mrs. Bailey was, however, uneasy enough about Dr Fellowes' new prescriptions for Alex to bring the subject up with her husband that evening. Ephraim's reaction was not what she hoped for.

"I always said it," her husband said, in between forkfuls of steaming shepherd's pie. "But Dr. Clarke would not agree. I don't know why not. A boy should be out of doors. It's his natural place."

"A healthy boy should be out of doors. But Alexander is not healthy. The scarlet fever is still in him, only waiting to erupt again." Mrs. Bailey knew nothing of medical matters, but she feared that her husband might come around to the opinion that Alex would live to adulthood. "I fear you may be given false hope by this doctor, Ephraim. I would not have you hurt." She added quickly.

"Poor Alexander! It is a tragedy to be taken so young, but - "

"Lydia, he's not dead yet! Even if this should hasten things, I'm of the opinion that he should get out and enjoy fresh air, sun, and perhaps friends his own age. How did I not insist on that before now? Dr. Fellowes' plan is quite right! I agree with it! And if our boy has not long to live, let him enjoy what's left to him."

She said no more. *'Our boy'*! What a fool he was! *His* boy!

"Good hearty vittles," said her husband then. "Do you send this up to the nursery to Alexander? No? You should. It would build him up in no time. What does he get?"

"Broth and bread," she said mechanically. "An invalid diet."

Alex went to visit the Fellowes family the following Saturday, and he returned with cheeks glowing and a happy expression. After that, he received invitations to go out and about with them, and gradually became accustomed to being a part of a group of children in the neighbourhood, older and younger, boys and girls. Mrs. Bailey watched for signs of a relapse, and to her satisfaction had not long to wait until Alexander became ill again.

He awoke one morning with a high fever. She called Dr. Fellowes, mostly to show him that she had been right and he, the professional man, wrong. But he took no notice of her as she railed against his going out and about in all weathers. It rained the other day, and he was caught out in it. That, she was sure, was where Alex got the fever from, and she was sure it must be very serious, possibly even the dreaded lung inflammation or the beginning of consumption. Dr. Fellowes followed her into the nursery and laid his bag on the sofa where the boy was lying. Nurse Wren was dipping linens in a basin to bathe his forehead.

"Now, Alexander, you're not feeling well this morning? Open your mouth and say 'AAAH.' Good lad! Well now. if it isn't the measles coming on. Mrs. Bailey, he's got the measles like Calloway and his young sister. Were you playing with them recently, Alexander? On Tuesday? There we have it. Keep his fever down and feed him an invalid diet and he will be well again in a few days."

"Measles!" Mrs. Bailey stormed.

"Yes, the more he mixes with other children, the more he will bring home. It's best he gets all these childhood illnesses behind him when he's young. When he's better, I'll inoculate him against smallpox. I saw in his chart that it has never been done."

"Diseases! He'll bring home diseases! Doctor Fellowes, I must protest his ever going out again! How am I to protect my own son?"

The door had opened, and Ephraim was standing there. Everybody present now understood the way it was. She pursed her lips in a stubborn manner, turned, and flounced out of the room, her face red with fury or embarrassment at having shown her heart, or perhaps both.

There was silence that evening at dinner. Not even the perfectly-cooked roast beef and Yorkshire pudding could draw a compliment from Ephraim Bailey. He seemed detached from the food and ate mechanically without saying a word. Mrs. Bailey was trying to be her pleasant self, the flirty woman she had been when they had first met, but he did not respond. Something had altered, and she too lapsed into a quiet and angry silence.

In his home, Dr. Fellowes related to his wife what had taken place as she pounded a cake of bread dough on the kitchen table.

"I had better keep an eye on that child," he said. "It's clear to me that she resents him."

"Oh, Basil, surely she wouldn't try to harm him."

"She is not going to try to help him. I will not forget the look in her eyes. Not a trace of affection. Nurse Wren has given enough hints to allow me to suspect the true state of affairs, and now I can see it for myself. She has banked on Alexander dying and her own child inheriting the land. I was in company with some men at the pub, and it's well known that the Livingstones feel very cheated. It's not unusual for a second wife to favour her own over the rightful heir. The world has more Agrippinas than you think. A lot of them do it with arsenic, slow poisoning.

Not that I think she would stoop to that," he hastily added.

"Who," said Mrs. Fellowes with some amusement as she turned the floury dough, "is Agrippina when she's at home?"

"The Emperor Nero's mother. She made sure he got the throne, though he was not the heir. As for the rightful heir, the son of Emperor Claudius, he suffered a hasty dispatch."

CHAPTER 9

DR FELLOWES

Alexander continued to thrive. The childhood illnesses beyond him, he put on weight, and his muscles became stronger with the exercises prescribed by Dr. Fellowes. By the time he was ten years old, his stepmother was seriously worried that Clarence would be deprived, after all, of what she was sure was his birthright. Ephraim was taking Alexander about the farm, teaching him about the sheep, the pigs, and the cattle. He had been to market in Carlisle, and he was even beginning to talk like the farmer he was intended to be. His speech included words like shearing, shoats, and market price.

Something had to be done. Whereas in the past, she had thought that neglect would be enough, but it was obvious now that an intervention of some sort would have to take place.

That would be murder, she said to herself, but her heart was so set on her own ambitions and on those of her son, that the boy Alexander began to lose his humanity in her eyes. Alex was a parasite, in the way, inconvenient, with no right to life itself.

How to act without being caught? Dr. Fellowes was, of course, in the way also. His care, his vigilance, his scrutiny of herself.

She did have a way to get rid of him, at least.

Mrs. Fellowes often said that it was her ambition that they should move to Leeds, for they both hailed from there, and crags and lakes were nothing to her, and the sight of so many sheep, for miles and miles, made her cross-eyed. Give her a thriving city with shops and playhouses! Her husband would find a position there someday, and they would be glad to remove there, and be near her old mother too.

"Father," said Mrs. Bailey one winter day as they walked in the snowy maze of holly trees in front of the house. It was a good place to converse without being heard. "Do you know anybody of influence in Leeds? Somebody who could offer Dr. Fellowes a post? A prestigious post, perhaps? An offer it would be difficult to turn down?"

"Oh, is it that important?" Mr. Livingstone was aware of her concern.

"Grandfather would think so," was Lydia's reply. "If we are to get the land back. He's in the way, Papa. Dr. Fellowes. Dr. Clarke was our man, without even being aware of it. I think Dr. and Mrs. Fellowes would benefit from a change of air," she went on with satisfaction. "She is always harping on about returning to Leeds. Why do we not try to grant her wish?"

"Oh, I see. Well, my dear, if that's what you want me to do, I shall pay Dr. Gordon a call the next time I go to Leeds. He knows the chief medical officer of the hospital there."

Nothing more had to be said. Dr. Fellowes received a very surprising offer in the post, and he was gratified and pleased to accept it. His wife was ecstatic, and they left within a short time.

The people of Stagtarn were sorry to see him go. He was a good man, and kind.

He was replaced by Dr. Clarke's nephew, Dr. Short. Mrs. Bailey decided there was no necessity for him to see Alexander at all. She said so to her husband.

"He has improved greatly!" Ephraim said, tucking into roast beef. "I have no anxieties for him now. In fact, I am going to send him away to school."

School! In school, he would be out of her control. What was to happen? There were only two months in which she had to think of something.

CHAPTER 10

MUSHROOMS

Walking in the wood gathering blackberries one September day, Mrs. Bailey espied some mushrooms growing around the base of a tall tree. She bent to examine them.

They were not of the edible variety. When was the cook's day off? She had been asking to go and see her sick aunt, and Mrs. Bailey thought it time to grant her request and she sent her away for three days.

She went out again and gathered the mushrooms. At home, she hid them in a box in her dressing room.

Alexander still ate his meals in the nursery with his half-brother Clarence and his young sister, so the day after sending the cook away and after giving Nurse Wren an unexpected evening off, she prepared a stew of the mushrooms. and mixing them with some roasted mutton and potatoes, brought dinner to the nursery herself.

"I want some mushrooms!" Clarence asked, seeing his brother apparently favoured over him.

"No, dear, your stomach is too delicate," Mrs. Bailey said. The young boy threw a tantrum, and two-year old Maria screamed in support, but her mother put her foot down, something she rarely did with her own children.

"They taste funny," Alexander said after a few forkfuls.

"That's the herb I put into it. But you have to eat it. I went to a lot of trouble to get them for you, because they're good for the blood."

Alexander ate them, grimacing and making faces, but then he suddenly vomited them all, making a dreadful mess she had to clean up all by herself, for she did not want Nurse Wren to find out what he had had to eat. She was angry, and she made Alexander feel bad for becoming sick and causing her all that trouble, so she made him help clean it up too. All the while she was thinking, *I tried to kill my stepson.* She could hardly believe it of herself.

Nurse Wren returned to find the nursery in order and all of her charges tucked up in bed, and Mrs. Bailey gave her a glass of wine to enjoy, as 'a treat, because I know you work very hard, very hard indeed,' and told her to turn in early.

Alex was weak the following morning and could not eat anything. Nurse Wren soon found out, for he told her himself what had made him ill.

"And, was Master Clarence sick also?"

"No, Mama just gave it to me, for my blood, she said." Alex replied innocently. Nurse Wren suspected immediately but told herself that what she was thinking could not be true, though she did talk of it in the village, how Master Alexander ate bad mushrooms, given to him by his stepmother while she and the cook were away.

Their father, however, would hear of it. Mrs. Bailey thought it wise to tell him before someone else did.

"Where did he get those mushrooms?" he asked.

"I don't know. They were in the larder. I thought them perfectly safe. When the cook comes back, I shall ask her."

Instead, Mrs. Bailey wrote to the cook telling her not to come back, enclosing two weeks wages.

"I have had a letter from the cook," she said to Mr. Bailey, in a vexed tone of voice. "She wishes to stay with her aunt, and she will not be returning. Now I shall have to find another, and at short notice..."

"Very inconvenient," Ephraim said vaguely, but domestic matters did not really concern him, as long as she could cook hearty meals for a man out of doors all day long.

She soon found another cook, a rather clueless girl she could train up herself.

Her next attempt had to be a well-planned, well-executed operation, but it would have to wait until Christmas or even next summer, for Alex was going away to school.

A sense of guilt tore her heart at times, but she chased it resolutely away. Her son, a Livingstone, was going to return the estate to those to whom it rightfully belonged. There was no other way. She blamed God. She had married Mr. Bailey in the full expectation of Alex being carried to his reward. Innocent little child that he was, it would have been the best thing for him. But God had tricked her and made him better, all the more to plague her and to tempt her to do things that were wrong. It was not her fault at all. She could not drop her claims, and that of her family, for the sake of righteousness. That was the sole reason for her marriage to Ephraim Bailey. It was her duty, she argued to herself. Alexander was in the way.

Her father was in agreement with her, every step of the way.

"I could not attempt this without your help, Papa," she often said to him as they walked together in the holly trees.

Mrs. Bailey soon found out that she had another friend also. Her father often called to Reginald Turnbull, the owner of the newly built Reginald Inn, a bachelor, and on her first visit there she found herself attracted to this well-made, handsome man, with regular features, deep set grey eyes and a cleft chin. He about the same age as her. The proper thing to do would be to avoid him, but she was bored with Ephraim, and she made it a habit to call whenever she was in the village, on some pretext or other, driving her own chariot. He was far below her in rank, but she disregarded that. He might be useful. She wanted Reginald Turnbull to adore her.

CHAPTER 11

SECOND ATTEMPT

Mrs. Bailey fleetingly considered arsenic. It was a tasteless powder. It was used on the farm for treating infestations in the sheep's wool. It would be easy to obtain, only she never went to the farm offices. She balked at it, not so much because doctors were now able to examine dead bodies for signs of arsenic poisoning, but because it would cause suffering to the boy. There was no need for that. She did not hate him, and she did not know how she could endure the guilt of seeing him in pain, and it was a nasty, prolonged affair. And Nurse Wren! She feared her, so there would be no poisoning. She was almost glad the mushrooms hadn't worked.

Reginald Turnbull soon knew of her frustration. He was deeply in love. They often went to an empty room upstairs. She thought the rooms dull and dingy and told him so, and advised him on the décor, which resulted in the housekeeper giving notice, so he engaged another and spent money he did not have on redecorating. Lydia was pleased, but to avoid prying eyes in the inn they sometimes met in secluded spots on the moors in summer.

"So, when you married into Stagtarn Hall, you really thought Alexander was going to die?" he asked her one afternoon.

"He was dying. But there was a miracle of sorts, and he began to recover."

"It looks as if you simply have to put up with the situation," he said to her.

"Oh no," she said immediately. "I am not putting up with the situation."

"But what do you propose to do about it?"

"Accidents happen," she said, giving him a long look. He frowned.

"That is out of the question, Lydia."

"What do you mean?"

"Why did you look at me like that?"

"Because I thought you might wish to assist me."

" Do you want me to hang?"

"No, you would not hang. Nobody hangs for accidents."

"He's a child."

"He's sixteen. Hardly a child now. He has ruined my life, and my son's life. How can I have my own child ruined?"

"Clarence would hardly be poor. He can have a profession, the military or the navy, perhaps. Or go into your father's business, the mills."

"No, the land belongs to us. We will have it back. Don't you understand, Reggie? Don't you?"

"Oh, my love, do not weep, I am sorry."

"It's not fair! It should never have become theirs, and we want it back!"

"Is there not any other way? Would not your husband be persuaded that Alexander must be passed over on account of his having been unhealthy, and that it would be too much for him?"

"Oh no, he would not allow that. But never mind. I shall see to it myself, and not involve you."

He was silent, and she was weepy. She put a distance between them and parted from him in ill-humour.

It took a few meetings, and several shows of petulance and unhappiness, for him to come around to the idea that he would assist her.

CHAPTER 12

THORA TARN

Alexander loved the water, and there were lakes galore to satisfy him. His favourite was Thora Tarn, a small lake that lay in a valley surrounded by rocky hillsides with a family of high stones, like a group of six rock giants, near the water. They were ancient. The locals called them 'the Brothers of Thora.'

Though he had friends at school whose homes he visited and who sometimes came to stay with him, he was happiest on his own. He had spent most of his young childhood relying on his capacity to amuse himself, and on school holidays, when he could be spared from the farm, he walked or rode long distances around the area, enjoying the absolute quiet, and finally sat to read a book and eat an apple or a piece of bread he'd brought with him.

On summer days, he stripped off his clothes and dove into the cold, pristine waters. One day, while in the middle of the lake, he observed the figure of a man standing on the rocks at the shoreline. It was quite strange he should come all the way out to this spot. He was a little annoyed, because people did not often come here, as there was a superstition about it. He did not believe in Thora, or her giant brothers, for that matter.

He was too far away to make out any feature at all. He supposed that the man had happened by, and seeing the swimmer, wondered if he should stay around in case he was in trouble. Alex began to swim toward him, to show the man that he was all right, but to his surprise the figure took off almost at a run, up among the Brothers of Thora, and was to be seen no more. There was a scattering of shepherd's cottages about the hillsides, but this man was not a shepherd.

He had left his clothes on a rock, and he dressed quickly, his curiosity now piqued. But there was no sign of the man. Alex shrugged and forgot the incident and resumed his enjoyment of the spot and the sunny day.

A quarter of a mile away, Reggie Turnbull paused for breath. He had followed Alex today on his horse, keeping to a path above him, out of sight but watching him, as he strode on the lower elevations near the lake. He still did not know how he was to carry out what his lover expected of him, but it would not be too difficult if Master Alexander had the habit of going off on his own to isolated spots. But to make everything look like an accident, that would be the challenge. And, of course, the body would have to be found, to prove his demise. Lydia would be happy then. The way would be clear for Clarence. She would be at peace, and Reggie was sure that one day, after Mr. Bailey's demise, which could also happen sooner than later, that she would become Mrs. Reginald Turnbull. He would then move to the hall. He had every right to expect that, for her third child, a daughter named Lily, was his.

He had to hurry back now, for his business was being neglected, and the employees were lazy when he was not there. His horse was tethered at a grassy spot in the shade, and he quickly reached her.

CHAPTER 13

THE ATTEMPT

Alexander's father was indulgent with him on his holidays. Some mornings he helped him on the farm, and others he was free to go and do as he pleased.

"What are you doing today, Alexander?" Mrs. Bailey asked him every morning at breakfast.

"If Father doesn't need me, I shall go for a walk," he replied.

"You are free, but I will need you in the afternoon in the shearing shed," his father replied.

"May we ask where you are walking to?" was her next question.

"Oh, wherever the fancy takes me," Alex said, stuffing an apple into his pocket.

"I declare, if you ever go missing, Alexander, we won't know where to look! He should at least tell us where he goes, Ephraim."

"Yes, your mother is right. Tell us where you're going."

"I thought I'd climb Moss Crag and then go for a swim."

"It's dangerous to swim on your own," his stepmother said. To herself, she found herself lamenting later, *'I warned him, I warned him not to swim on his own! Oh, the foolish boy! Why did he not listen to me?'*

"Don't go out of your depth," said his father. "And avoid Moses Water, for there can be currents there in high winds."

"There's only a breeze today, Father. But no, I shall not go there."

"Where will you swim today, Alexander?" his stepmother persisted.

There is another water beyond that, Thora," he replied.

"What, you are not afraid of her?" his father joked.

"No, Father. Thora does not disturb me." Alex chuckled.

That was the end of the conversation as they went their separate ways for the day.

Reginald Turnbull was in his office when a sealed note came, delivered by a footman from the hall, who was cross at Madam demanding he go and tell Mr. Turnbull that Mr. Bailey wanted extra horses next week. Why send a note when he could deliver the message in person? He did not believe her, and he was unwilling to be the messenger of a planned immoral tryst. Mr. Turnbull took the sealed, scented envelope from him in a rather awkward manner, turned away, and opened it.

'This morning. Thora Tarn. Hurry.'

"Is there any reply, sir?" Smithers asked with a little sarcasm.

"No, no message."

"About the horses, sir?"

"Oh, yes, I shall have as many as three available, I expect. There is no need to write a note about it. You may go."

"I have business in Stoney Mill," he said to Pete, his senior man, referring to the next village. "I'll be gone a few hours. It's a good day, and I think I will walk."

"Very good, Mr. Turnbull," Pete replied. They all knew what his 'business' could be, something to do with Mrs. Bailey. He thought nobody knew, but they all did. Another morning free of the boss.

His plan was easy enough. He would strike the boy on the head with a rock from above, and drag him, unconscious or dead to the lakeside. It would look as if he'd struck his head on a rock, possibly when he dived in, and been washed ashore. He'd have to strip him and leave his clothes on the place where he was supposed to have gone in.

He was nervous as he followed Alex, and he was very hot from walking quickly to catch him up, for the young man was going at a good pace. He wished he was mounted, but his horse could give him away. His heart thudded. What if it went wrong? What if there was blood on Alex's shirt? How could that be explained? He'd have to wash it. It was very complicated! Should he wait until Alex was ready to dive before he struck him? The whole thing seemed very muddled. He was too nervous.– If Alex saw him, and lived, it would be all up with him. Penal Servitude breaking stones in a quarry. If he died, and it all came out, he'd hang. Lydia would deny that she'd put him up to it. He would not implicate her either.

While his thoughts ran on in this fashion, Alex had passed the Brothers, reached a large rock that overhung the lake, and was evidently going to dive from there into the water. He was stripping off his outer garments.

There was no time now. Dodging into the safety of the Brothers to think of how he ought to proceed, Turnbull paused a moment. He heard the splash. Alex had already gone into the water.

It was not going to work, but how could he face Lydia? How many more times would he have to follow this youth before an opportunity arose? He couldn't do this for the entire summer. His determination rose to do it today.

He would have to go in too. He, too, was a swimmer, a strong one. He slid into the water and trying to make no sound, followed Alex. When he reached him, he grasped his legs and dragged him under, and pushed him down, holding his breath as long as he could, but he was out of breath. All that walking had done him in. Then through the muffled sounds of the water and the splashes as Alex tried to free himself, he thought he heard a dog bark. It made him panic, and he let go. He needed to make his own escape now. Hopefully the lake would do the rest of the work for him. He reached the bank and hauled himself up. Glancing behind, he saw no sign of Alexander Bailey. He hurried upon his way. He had left him alive, but he would not be able to recover himself sufficiently to save himself. With a bit of luck, the body would be washed up. If not, perhaps the lake would be dragged. He did not look back, but rather he ran for the safety of the Brothers.

CHAPTER 14

THE GOOD SHEPHERD

Alex had felt hands upon his ankles, and he felt himself drawn under. His lungs filled with lake water, and all was dark and turbulent around him. He did not see the person pulling him down, but the presence was strong, stronger than he. Then the attacker left, and he was alone, his lungs bursting. He had entered a space of brown murkiness and was being propelled along through no will of his own, the lake had its grip upon him and was doing with him as she wished. But he fought to come to the surface and gasped for breath. Perhaps all was not lost! He tried to float himself on top of the water but felt himself going down again. He rose again, floundering, but sank. He could not breathe. He knew that if he went down a third time, it would be the end of him.

He was suddenly aware of strong hands pulling him into shallow water and he was laid on the side of the lake, on the rocks, where he coughed up and also vomited quantities of lake water.

"What weer you doin' in the water, lad? There's a wicked un in the tarn, ther is! Did she pull ye down?" It was a shepherd, his hair wild and white, his face tanned and furrowed, the few teeth left to him brown from tobacco, but with a look of plain, country kindness about him. A sheepdog was at his side.

It was some time before he could reply.

"No, I don't know."

"Ye best lie here for a time, until yer ready to go on yer way. Oh my, look at your leg there, cut open, it is. Some sharp stones 'ere."

"Did you see anybody else here?" Alex spluttered.

"I saw something move in the Brothers, right by here, but I thought it was my little ewe, but the movement was so quick, it might have been a man."

"That man tried to drown me."

"Oh, no, that was Thora. She was pullin' you into 'er cave, that one, but I caught you first, thank God. I saw your 'ead come up and bob down again."

The lake was said by the shepherds to be inhabited by the ghost of an unfortunate girl named Thora, who in ancient times had thrown herself in after her lover had jilted her. Her brothers had run down to save her, but they were too late, and not wanting to go home and tell their mother, they had stayed by the lake and turned to stone.

"How came you to pass by?" Alex struggled to ask, but he was beginning to breathe easier.

"I never come this way, but one of my sheep is lost, and I'm looking for 'er. I was walking along by the edge of th'water, hoping Thora didn't get 'er. I'll bind up that leg of yours. If you'll try to stand, and lean on me, my cottage isn't far."

Alex tried to rise, helped by the shepherd.

CHAPTER 15

LYDIA

The bell rang for lunch, and Mr. and Mrs. Bailey took their seats at table. She saw at once that Alex's chair was empty.

"He's late," said Ephraim.

"I suppose he's in no hurry, this fine weather. We will start, Maggie," Lydia said.

"Very well, Madam."

At two o'clock, there was still no sign of Alexander. Mrs. Bailey had been almost too nervous to eat but had forced herself to empty her plate as usual. Ephraim said he would give Alex a talking-to when he did arrive, and he went out again.

Three o'clock struck. Mrs. Bailey could not keep her mind on her tapestry. The time dragged. At four, when the sun was moving around the side of the house, tea was served.

Four o'clock! Every passing minute was telling her that Alexander was no more.

"Maggie, could you send word to Mr. Bailey that Mr. Alexander is not back yet?"

"Very well, Madam. Where could he be, Madam? He's never been out as long as this. He must be very 'ungry by now."

"He said he was going for a swim, Maggie, and I am not happy that he went alone. I hope nothing has happened to him." Mrs. Bailey thought it no harm to begin her part in the narrative of how foolish Alexander was to go swimming alone.

"Oh, Madam, you mustn't think th'worst; it's likely he lay down and fell asleep i'the sun."

Mrs. Bailey put down her tapestry and walked back and forth. Her heart was beginning to burst with excitement. Next to the birth of her son, this was the most significant day of her life. Alex was missing! Gone out of her life! She almost felt like running upstairs and changing into a bright, colourful gown instead of this dull plaid, and putting on her best jewellery. But she could not do that, of course. Her joy had to be kept to herself.

The Livingstone inheritance was within reach at last! But she needed some definite news. If only Reggie would send a message! She went to the window, her eyes on the long avenue to the gate, hoping to see one of his employees come.

"Come on, Reggie, come, come." She found herself saying aloud, and as if in answer to her command a figure came around the bend in the avenue.

Reggie! No! One of his men with a message? The avenue was long, and she had to wait. It was agonizing.

A tall, fair haired youth, head down, bedraggled and limping was making his way to the house.

She could not believe her eyes.

It was Alexander. No, she was dreaming. It could not be! It could not! But the figure was getting larger. It was he! Alive! Alive and coming home!

She turned, gasping for breath, suddenly terrified. That he had suffered some injury was beyond doubt, but what had happened? Had he seen Reginald? What did he know? Why did Reginald not get some message to her that he had failed? Where was Reginald?

Her face went deathly pale, and she sat suddenly in a chair. Every limb was weak, her heart seemed to fade away in her breast, the room swam about her.

Maggie entered the room, smiling broadly. "Madam, you may rest easy, for Mr. Alexander is coming up th'path. Madam! You look as if you 'ave seen a ghost! What could be th'matter?" She bustled away, saying something about smelling salts.

Alexander entered the drawing room, and at first, she could not look at him. A blanket of disbelief, horror, and guilt descended upon her. She could not look him in the eye but turned her face away. She clasped and unclasped her hands, her tapestry at her feet.

"Mother?" Alex said.

"You are injured!" was all she could manage. She was saved from saying any more by her husband rushing into the room.

"Where were you?" he asked his son with more anger than concern.

As he sat down in a chair and told his alarming story, that someone had tried to drag him under. Mrs. Bailey managed to compose herself. 'Someone.' No recognition, then! She felt better and was able to speak to him quite rationally, with caring in her voice. She even took up her tapestry again and was calm enough to try to use her needle.

"The other day when I was swimming at the lake, a man stood on the bank and watched me," he said then.

Again, no recognition. She was beginning to breathe with more normality. The blow was crushing, but it could have been worse. Much worse.

At the Reginald Inn, Mr. Turnbull waited for news that Master Alexander was missing; such news would not be contained for long. But no news came. Night fell. Stagtarn's tavern was open, and he ambled down there to hear if there was any news. There, he heard that Master Alexander had nearly drowned at Thora Tarn, but a shepherd had pulled him out just in time. This was not good news. Reggie had to worry if this shepherd had seen him. He was even more worried two days later when the magistrate's carriage passed through the village and stopped to ask the quickest way to Stagtarn Hall. Why was the magistrate going to Stagtarn? Was there something to investigate?

He felt sick to his stomach, and he knew he would not see Lydia for a few weeks. It would not be good for them to be seen together. He watched anxiously for the magistrate's carriage to come back. It did, but it went straight by the inn without stopping. He watched the back of it go, the hooves and rattles growing more faint with every second, and he began to feel easier.

Summer drew to a close. Autumn came. At last, he and Lydia met. It was then he learned that Alexander had reported that he had been dragged down by a man, but he did not know who it was.

"We are safe," Lydia said, her hand on his arm. "But we might not have been, had he seen you, and survived."

There was a reproach there, and it made him feel less of a man in her eyes.

“If that shepherd had not been there –“ he began.

“If you had gone about it in a different way – “ she pointed out. “You told me you would make sure he was gone. You put us in grave danger. The magistrate, however, felt it must have been some underwater weeds that my stepson got himself tangled in, and he did not feel it necessary to find and interview the shepherd. It was badly done of you, Reggie."

It stung. But Lydia put her arms about him, and it was as it had been before.

CHAPTER 16

THE BIG ORDER

PRESTON, LANCASHIRE

1852

"Tess, I have good news today," said her mother excitedly as she returned home from school one day in May. She was eleven years old now, and could read and write very well, knew all the principal capital cities of the world and all the about the Tudors and the Stuarts, and many other things. She had come to love school at last, and had friends there, one of whom was the schoolmaster's daughter Frances, and Frances' cousin whose father was an attorney's clerk. Her mother greatly encouraged these friendships, and when the girls gave each other little gifts at Christmas and on birthdays, she made sure that her daughter made beautiful little purses, collars, or lace handkerchiefs, perfectly stitched and elegantly embroidered. She often worked on the embellishments herself.

One of these gifts, a lace handkerchief given to the attorney's girl, was shown to a visitor, Mrs. Baddelley, whose husband owned three cotton mills in as many Lancashire towns. They were on their way to becoming the wealthiest people in the district and had built an ostentatious house on the outskirts of Preston. Mrs. Baddelley wanted to see more of Mrs. Woods' work, for she guessed it was the work of the mother, and called to see her one day. Before she left, she had engaged her to make a morning gown for her, and she was so pleased with the expertise that she engaged her to make her daughter's wedding gown. For this, Mrs. Baddelley recommended that she work on the gown in her home, for looking about her, she did not fancy the idea of expensive satins and silks coming to this little room that the Woodses called home, so the work was to be completely done at Baddelley Hall, as they had named their house.

"And as it's summer, and you will have school holidays, you are to come with me." Mrs. Woods declared. "I can teach you as I work. She has promised us a sunny room, and a very large table. Miss Baddelley will be there, of course, for fittings."

"Mama, if there are patterns, how will you manage them?"

Mrs. Woods had a great eye for measuring, and she used chalk on the material to be cut. The 'rock of eye,' learned from her father, meant that she had the skill of estimating the size of her client with her eyes, and that was followed by cutting, draping, and pinning. She did not use patterns. 'Rock of eye' had worked very well with the morning gown. She had no qualms.

As the Baddelleys had spared no expense on their house, they now spared no expense on Meredith's gown, nor upon her wedding, due to take place in the Hall on September 7th next. Mr. Baddelley had many new business friends and acquaintances, some of them quite important men, and the family was determined to make a splash. They were all of them to attend, even the younger children, and all were getting new clothes.

The following month, Mrs. Woods and Teresa walked up the hill to Baddelley Hall and went to the back door, where they were shown to the drawing room by a neat parlour maid. Mrs. Baddelley showed them to the room chosen to be the sewing room.

To their surprise, there were a few people there already.

"We are to make the men's suits first," Mrs. Baddelley informed her.

Mrs. Woods was pleased. She knew that work very well from her father's trade.

But then her heart sank when she saw Miss Deuville at a table with several rolls of brown paper and scissors, deep in conversation with two other people. She was talking of the rolls of paper.

Mrs. Baddelley left the room.

"I hope we can stay well away from her," Mrs. Woods murmured, nodding in Miss Deuville's direction. "If I didn't need the money, I'd be off, but how can I turn down a job like this? If Mrs. Baddelley is pleased with me, I will get more work from her friends."

It was to get even more alarming. Miss Deuville was in charge of the enterprise.

Unfortunately for Mrs. Woods, Miss Deuville announced to the room that paper patterns were going to be made and used. "It is more scientific than the old method," she said. "You will measure the body. Mr. Watts will measure the men, and you, Mrs. Woods, the women, and write down all the measurements in a book with the person's name on it, and you will then draft a pattern, cut out the pattern from the paper, with all the measurements noted carefully upon it, and we shall not deviate from it, not even to one sixteenth of an inch. I do not want to see anybody using the rock of eye."

This caused great uneasiness to Mrs. Woods.

"I often thought of asking you to teach me 'ow to read and write," she said quietly to Tess. "But you had enough to do. It didn't seem fair to you. How will I manage now?"

"I'll help you, Mama. But do you even have a proper measuring tape? We'll have to get one, we will." Tess looked about and among the sewing things on a side table, was a measuring tape. She snatched it up. "I won't leave your side, I promise."

CHAPTER 17

PERQUISITES

There was one benefit to the Baddelley sewing that Tess noticed. Her mother became less strict with her, and at times she treated her like a friend or an ally. Tess realised that as she could read and write, her mother depended on her. It was a strange feeling. Her mother had whipped her out the door to school, and now her education gave her advantages over her. It made her feel humble, grateful, and protective all at the same time, for she saw in Miss Deuville someone who could humiliate and mistreat her mother, and she made sure to be attentive to her. Mr. Watts measured Mr. Baddelley and his two sons, Mrs. Woods measured all the females with her daughter's assistance, and made the patterns and after that, everybody got to sewing.

"What wonderful work," Mrs. Baddelley gushed one day to Mrs. Woods as she embroidered a black satin waistcoat for Mr. Baddelley with silk thread in the same colour. "I have never seen anything like it." She passed on to Miss Deuville's table, where she asked her if she thought perhaps the cravat was a little too small for her boy? Miss Deuville reddened and said that large cravats for boys were out of fashion, and this was what the Parisian *garçons* were wearing, but if Madame wanted Master Adam to have a large cravat, she would make a large cravat of course. She only had to say, it was Madame's choice. Mrs. Baddelley harrumphed and passed on to the next table to where Mr. Watts was cutting out cloth, telling him that Master John was broader in the shoulders than one would think and that though he had been measured, he should be measured a second time.

"What an interfering woman," muttered Mr. Watts, after she had left, and Miss Deuville nodded vigourously. They both glanced at Mrs. Woods and then at each other. The glance did not pass Tess' attention. She felt a little anxious.

That evening she saw her mother pocket a square foot of waste satin left from the waistcoat.

"Mama, don't," she said, aghast.

"Why not? It's a perquisite of dressmaking. This is of no use to anybody."

"But you should ask Mrs. Baddelley, all the same!"

"Bother 'er with a little thing like that? No, for I saw Miss Deuville slip a card of gilt buttons into her reticule. If she can do it, I can."

Tess could not rest easy. Her mother was leaving herself open to accusations of theft. Dreading what was to happen, she saw Miss Deuville bear down upon them, her tall gaunt frame appearing to tower over them.

"I think you shall do plain work from now on, Mrs. Woods," she said in her affected French accent. "While Madame does not see any fault in that embellishment, I do. I have a trained eye, yes, a very trained eye, to see the smallest flaw, the tiniest mistake, and here, this stitch here, has a tiny, tiny loop."

"As you say, Miss Deuville." Mrs. Woods sounded smug for all of her humble words.

But Mrs. Baddelley reversed the decision in the morning. She preferred Mrs. Woods' fancy work to Miss Deuville's. The latter was very put out, muttering for a time about newly rich people who had neither refinement nor taste, and when she was lady-in-waiting to the countess in Monte Carlo, she was very content. There was class, there was taste.

Even Mr. Watts raised his eyebrows at this, and Tess and her mother tried not to laugh. Lady-in-waiting indeed!

The summer went on. The suits were made, and then the wedding gown materials came from Bond Street.

By now, Teresa's mother and Miss Deuville were at war, but a silent one so as not to draw attention to themselves.

"Mrs. Woods, you will assist me in the cutting out of the sleeves. Here is the book of Miss Baddelley's measurements. You will call them out to me while I check the pattern."

Tess was instantly by her mother's side, for Miss Deuville probably knew that her mother could not read, and Miss Deuville's handwriting was very fancy, all twirls and full of embellishments so that the numbers were scarcely readable.

"Go and finish the seam on Miss Georgina's petticoat, Thereze." Miss Deuville said angrily, mispronouncing her name.

Teresa found the relevant page and whispered the measurements to her mother before obediently going to her table.

Nobody was quite sure what happened next, whether Mrs. Woods had not heard Tess properly, or as Miss Deuville alleged, she wished to deliberately sabotage her, but the expensive silk was cut too narrow and short.

Mrs. Baddelley blamed Miss Deuville, as she was in charge. The former lady-in-waiting had hysterics. The housekeeper, Mrs. Henley, was called, and she took her to her room and gave her tea to calm her down. There, Miss Deuville poured out all her troubles to a sympathetic Mrs.

Henley, and by the time she had finished talking, she was entirely persuaded by her. Miss Deuville returned to the workroom calmer and convinced that she had the housekeeper on her side. The work resumed, and all went without incident for a time.

But unknown to anybody in the workroom, Mrs. Baddelley was keeping all of her friends and her future in-laws apprised of how the sewing was coming along, and she formed the habit of criticising Miss Deuville. She had airs because she was foreign, and was bad-tempered and resentful of poor Mrs. Woods, a widow of extraordinary talent and workmanship, the like of which she had never seen. She had dressmaking in her little finger!

Almost the entire wardrobe was made, and then something unexpected happened.

Miss Deuville's dressmaking business began to lose orders, and Mrs. Woods found, to her surprise, that she was getting orders instead, some of them large and requiring that she hire help.

"I 'ave to think about you leaving school now," she exclaimed one evening to Tess, after they had had a visit from one of Mrs. Baddelley's neighbours asking her to make over a gown into a more fashionable style. "I will need your help!"

Tess was disappointed. She did not want to leave school and help her mother full-time making clothes! No more reading, no more writing, geography, or history; she had not realised how attached she had become to learning.

"But I thought you wanted me to stay in school, Mama!"

"You've had how many years now? Nearly six! That's enough for any girl. Your friends are going to boarding school, and do you want to be the only girl left in a class of boys? It looks as if I'm going to get a lot of business, and if I can't supply the work and in a timely way, they won't ask me again."

Her mother spoke the truth about her classmates. There were very few girls left. Most had gone to work at Miller's or Horrocks cotton mills, and any whose parents had money were sending them away to school.

I have to leave school then, she said glumly to herself.

"Miss Deuville isn't getting those orders," her mother said with exultation, "thanks to Mrs. Baddelley favouring *me*, her star is falling. I can't say I'm one bit sorry. Good enough for 'er, is what I say. A horrid woman."

Tess did not feel the same exultation or ease. She was frightened of the towering woman with the severe expression and who had taken a great dislike to them. Would she pack and leave Preston? Or would she try to get her business back, and harm them?

CHAPTER 18

THE ENEMY FALLS

The following day, Mrs. Woods was very surprised, and pleased, to find herself supervisor of the work at Baddelley Hall, for Miss Deuville had sent a note announcing that she would no longer proffer her services to Mrs. Baddelley.

"You mun stay by my side all day," she instructed Tess, "and write everything as usual, Oh how glad I am I ‘ad you educated! This evening, you will write a letter to Aunt Stowe. I will dictate it."

In the last few years, Mrs. Woods had become friendly again with her sister Belle Stowe. They wrote to each other, with Tess writing for her mother and reading the letter to her, and Mrs. Woods had named her and her husband Jim guardians of Teresa, should anything happen to her.

That evening, Tess wrote the letter her mother dictated. It was full of exultation and triumph, and it troubled her to write such words. Two days later, a reply came.

Dear Eliza, your letter alarmed me no end. You dont know what this woman mite do. You were rash before and please be on your gard. Jim is very worrit about you. We see all kinds of folks here in our place of business and some folks are bad. Be careful becose she mite have friends that will not be afeard to do you harm for a few shillings, such is her tipe. Be on the lookout always for her revenge.

Mrs. Woods laughed heartily at this response, but Teresa did not.

"What does she mean, you were rash before?"

"I suppose she means running off with your father." Her mother wiped tears of mirth from her eyes. "Miss Deuville will not try to do me in. She's too much of a coward. She'd hang. How I'd love to see her hang!"

"You'd be dead, Mama." Teresa was annoyed. Her mother's dislike of Miss Deuville had turned to a state of loving-to-hate. It frightened her. "I think you should take the advice of Aunt Belle."

"Oh, Belle. She's a sharp piece. She'd do exactly the same as me. And you're far too young to tell me what to do, Miss Tess. I'm going to take Miss Deuville's two girls and get them to work at Baddelleys. They're good girls and would get a lot done in a short time."

"Mama, you will make Miss Deuville even more angry!"

"Nonsense! I'll be doing 'er a favour, for she won't be able to afford to keep 'em on! What will they work on? She 'as no orders! Anyway, she's left Preston. I heard it at the butcher's. Make me a cuppa, Tess, I'm worn out from laughing. Oh, your father! He was so serious about everything! I'm afraid you take after him, always seeing trouble ahead."

"I barely remember Papa," Tess said, swinging the kettle over the fire.

"He took you to Mass one Christmas, and when he came home it seems you got up to mischief while he was up taking Communion," she said.

"Tell me! For I remember nowt really! He was tall, and 'andsome, and used to lift me up and call me Princess, but as for going to Mass, I don't remember, except there was a smell of incense, and candles lighting, and there was singing."

"He was highly amused. Do you remember Miss Hughes and Mr. Henderson? You were very disappointed that it was them singing, not angels." Tess didn't remember any of that.

Mrs. Woods was in a great mood for reminiscing, so she spoke at length. They drank tea as the light faded, and Tess hung on every word. They had many chats over the next few months, and Tess's fears for Miss Deuville's revenge began to abate. Work was plentiful. The wedding clothes were much admired at the society wedding in September, and even more work resulted from that.

The outcome was that Tess and her mother moved to a better house. Mrs. Woods deliberately chose the house in Meadow Street where Miss Deuville had her apartments, where she had been deliberately humbled whenever she took her work there. It was completely furnished and in a nice style. The front room caught the sun most of the day. It had a little fitting room with a long mirror behind a curtain, there was a wardrobe, chests of drawers, and two tables. Mrs. Woods, Teresa, and one of Miss Deuville's former apprentices did their day's work there. Behind that room were two smaller rooms, a living room, and a bedroom, and behind those the kitchen and scullery. There was no trace of its former occupant except for the red flocked wallpaper in the living room which she had chosen herself, and a painting on the wall that had evidently been forgotten.

The owner of the house, Mr. Nicholls, lived on the upper floor with his family. He was strict about the rent being on time, and Mrs. Woods promised she would have it for him every Thursday without fail.

Nobody knew where Miss Deuville had gone, and people who thought she was foreign speculated that she had 'gone back to France'.

To be able to take over the house of her arch-rival! She even had taken on one of the apprentices, Gwen. What a coup!

Mrs. Woods had also been able to employ a maid-of-all-work, Milly. She had never had a servant before. She took up residence in an attic room and was a good, hardworking girl.

CHAPTER 19

AUNT MYRTLE

The dingy room was in a back street in Blackpool, but it was all she could afford. It had light in the morning, and by this light the seamstress mended sheets and linens for the boarding houses. Some of them had holes so large that the guests must have put their feet through them. Of course, they were old sheets, threadbare, and it wouldn't take much to tear them. And the landladies expected her to patch them again! Only the cheapest places gave her work because she had come here without references. The hotels and snooty houses at the seafront had slammed their doors.

It was a far cry from running her own dressmaking business and mixing with her gentry clients. Miss Deuville, whose real name was Myrtle Matterson, was consumed with bitterness and plans to get revenge.

She had just read a letter from Preston with the gossipy news that Mrs. Woods, that wicked woman, had set up her own place of business, and in her former house at Meadow Street! It was unbearable news. She stood up and took a sheet, already torn badly, and rent it all the way down its length in anger, making a loud tearing sound.

"What is it, Aunt?" Her niece, Stella, was in the tiny scullery. She was a housemaid who was out of place at the moment and was helping Aunt Myrtle in return for her food and lodging.

"Aunt!" Stella stood in the doorway, alarmed. "What 'ave you done to that? They'll make you pay for it!"

"What do I care? Look at this letter I just got from Mrs. Henley at Baddelley Hall. She's the housekeeper, and the only person I had any time for at that house. Let us leave all this work, Stella, and take a long walk. I must tell you about how I came down in the world. It is all the fault of one Mrs. Woods..."

The walk was by the cliffs. A fresh breeze blew from the Irish Sea, but the women were so absorbed in their subject that they did not notice it.

"If I can help you in any way, I will," Stella pledged, an edge to her voice indicating her indignation at the unjust treatment of her aunt by all of Preston. "Ooh, I will! I will go and find her out, for as you say, she is not honest, and doesn't deserve her luck."

"She's even got herself a servant," Aunt Myrtle said bitterly. "She who hadn't a red penny in all the world only a few years ago. She had to scrimp and save to send that child to school. A servant! Stella, I have just had a thought pop into my head. With your help, and Eddie's, I might be able to take Mrs. Woods down a peg or two. I have a germ of an idea in my head. Will you help me? "

"I'm sure Eddie would go along with it. He's always on for something new. And when he hears what was done to you, Aunt, he'll drop everything. He hates his place anyway. The butler is a rotter, always looking over his shoulder. Family comes first."

CHAPTER 20

FAITH

The apprentice, Gwen, was a sweet girl about fifteen years old, and Tess found herself looking up to her. One day, Tess began to speak of her father and grandmother.

She put down her work, got up suddenly, and ran into the living room. She returned with a thick black leather bound book and opened it.

"There are the petals from the roses he picked for us, one day in summer. I don't really remember it. I was only four, but I've always known about and looked at the roses. Aren't they pretty? I love them. I wish I could remember him better, my father, and Grandma too."

"You'll be with them one day," Gwen said consolingly.

Mrs. Woods stared hard at her.

"I don't go fer any of that faith nonsense," she said.

But Tess' interest was piqued. She and Gwen began to talk together when Mrs. Woods was out. Gwen showed her the Bible. And Tess began to read it.

This is true, she thought to herself, after reading the Gospel of John. *It must be! If I could just read it to Mama! Why has she never heard this? Such love!*

But she was afraid to go to church on Sunday, either to Gwen's or to her own, St. Augustine's, the church where she knew she was baptised. That was Milly's church. Milly had made her First Communion and her Confirmation. But Tess had never gone to church after her father died, not since that Christmas she barely remembered.

A year passed, and then another. Tess was thirteen. Her mother was known as the best dressmaker for miles around. And then Mrs. Baddelley asked her to return to her home to make a new set of clothes, again, for a wedding. Their eldest son was about to marry the daughter of Lord Bonner-Smyth.

"You must have heard of Lord Bonner Smyth," gushed Mrs. Baddelley as she sat in the one elegant chair, reserved for visitors, in the sewing room at the Woods home. "My son was introduced to her when she visited her brother at Cambridge. He is friends with the young Lord. Their father has been dead for years now, so he holds the title and great lands, all around Oxfordshire. I shall want a very superior gown, Mrs. Woods. The bride is to wear blue, and the mother of the bride pink, and I have chosen lavender for myself, with a great deal of lace. Honiton, or Chantilly..."

Shortly after that, Milly left without notice. Nobody knew what had happened to her or where she had gone. A few days later, a knock came to the door, and a girl who was new in Preston said she was looking for domestic work, and she had heard from her enquiries that they might have a vacancy.

Her name was Stella Hobbs. She seemed pleasant and was very neat. She had good references, and they took her on.

Tess read the references. The handwriting on one was fancy and flourishing. As she had been little more than a child when she had accompanied her mother to Baddeleys for the first time, she did not recognise it. In any case, she had completely forgotten Miss Deuville, as had her mother.

CHAPTER 21

ANOTHER BIG ORDER

"You must be paying your maid something 'andsome," Mrs. Boyce remarked to Mrs. Woods one morning as she paid her a visit from her old neighbourhood. "I saw her walking out yesterday with a new hat, and I doubt I could afford as good as that for myself."

Contrary to her own fears or wishes, Mrs. Boyce was still hale and hearty, if a little suspicious of any 'scheme' now after the loss of one pound to her former neighbour's relatives. She came to Mrs. Woods for all of her sewing requirements, and she was happy not to be charged. The seamstress was trying to make up to her for her shady relations. Mrs. Woods had done well for herself, and she admired the widow and her growing daughter, of whom she was fond. But Mrs. Boyce feared Tess was plain, with sallow skin. Her father had foreign blood. And those ugly spots on her face! Not freckles, but a rash that seemed permanently there. It spoiled any looks she might have, and if it didn't clear up, no boy would look at her, though her eyes were nice enough. But she was obedient to her mother and treated everybody with respect. Her fancy work was admired everywhere. She could make lace to rival any in the big shops in Manchester or Liverpool.

"Stella gets the going rate," Mrs. Woods said in surprise, but not wanting to reveal how much she was paid, in case that was what Mrs. Boyce was really after. "But she has a follower, and I'm sure he must have made her a present of it."

"A follower! Are you going to allow followers?"

"She's eighteen years old. I wouldn't deny her a bit of fun. Besides, I know him. He's a footman up at Baddelley Hall, a nice lad."

Mrs. Woods liked Stella. She was pretty and neat as a pin, and the worst thing for a dressmaker was to have a slovenly maid going about in full view of the clientele. Stella herself was very good with her needle. She'd learned it from her mother, she said.

Mrs. Woods thought that the new footman at Baddelley Hall was sweet on Stella, for she had seen them walking one evening, their heads together, deep in conversation.

But how would a second footman afford to buy a fancy hat for his sweetheart? He had it bad!

Mrs. Woods made her way to Baddelley Hall soon afterwards, and was shown a great deal of expensive fabrics and laces, for, as Mrs. Baddelley said, her younger daughters now needed to be seen to advantage, because of all the important men there, and there was a certain widower who was very wealthy indeed, and was known to be on the lookout for a wife. There would be an age difference, but what did that matter? The wedding was to take place in the family seat in Oxford, a very large house, and there was to be a ball the evening of the wedding. Quite like royalty, was it not? Mrs. Woods stopped listening as she examined all the fine materials that the maid had taken from boxes, all carefully wrapped in yards and yards of tissue. It seemed even more important to Mrs. Baddelley to show the family off at this wedding than the last.

"This is particularly fine stuff, Madam," Mrs. Woods said, handling a length of yellow duchesse satin.

"That's for Georgiana's evening gown for the ball."

"With all due respect, Mrs. Baddelley, I must ask to be allowed to take some of this work home with me, for I have other clients, and must stay open." Mrs. Woods tone was firm, and Mrs. Baddelley understood her instantly, but asked if she would be willing to come up to the hall now and then in the evenings perhaps, and that was agreed to.

Though her primary intention in wanting to work in her own shop was to keep the business open and running, Mrs. Woods also thought that she would be able to filch her 'perks' easier at home than at Baddelley Hall. A remnant of this purple silk, a length of that white French muslin, a few feet of Valenciennes ribbon lace. all leftovers, of course. Tess would frown on that. Where did she get her scrupulous daughter?

CHAPTER 22

CHAT IN CARRIAGE

Christmas was coming as Mrs. Woods was putting the finishing touches to Miss Georgiana's evening gown. She and Tess worked until their eyes hurt on the fine stitching. While this was going on, Mrs. Woods was stuffing her 'perks' into a pink pillow case and putting them at the back of the wardrobe in her bedroom, usually when her daughter was not present to see her. She now had a fine bag of remnants. She would make caps, cravats, and fichus out of them, and offer them for sale in the window.

If only she had known that her secret was not a secret! Stella soon found the pillowcase, and she looked from time to time to see it grow with more fine stuffs.

The pillowcase, or pillowcases, as they would surely be soon, were not important. Bulging with material remnants would only point to her character. The plan that Miss Deuville had was far deeper, and Stella's footman friend was not her sweetheart, but her brother Eddie.

Every so often, Mrs. Woods had to visit Baddelley Hall for fittings, because her apartment would not hold more than four or five clients at a time, and it was simpler to take the garments to Baddelley Hall in a hansom cab, which Mrs. Baddelley paid for.

It was December 23rd. The last client had left, her new Christmas gown wrapped neatly in a parcel to bring home. Gwen gathered up the inevitable bits of materials and loose threads that littered every dressmaker's shop and tidied before she went home. Mrs. Woods and Tess wrapped themselves up in their cloaks, bonnets, and boots, and they carefully folded Miss Baddelley's yellow duchesse satin gown into a packet and left to hail a cab.

"We shall be home about seven, Stella, for our supper. We'll 'ave the fish soup from last night, and warm some bread in the oven for us, and bring the cheese in from the scullery to take the cold off. Come on, Tess."

“In a moment, Mama. I want to wear my new red bonnet.” Tess stopped to insert some holly into the green ribbon.

“Stella? Did you hear me?” Her mother’s voice sounded impatient.

"Yes, ma'am." Stella smirked behind their backs. If all went well, it would be one of the last nights that Mrs. Woods would spend in this house, this house that she had driven her aunt from.

"Oh, Mama, it's cold!" Tess shivered as she got into the cab, but she heard carol singing, and it made her forget the cold. What was it about the cheerfulness of those singers outside the emporium, all wrapped up snugly? They banished cold and darkness. Her heart lightened as she saw the shop windows still lit up and people strolling about, as mother and daughter made their way up to Baddelley Hall.

The Light shines in the Darkness, she had seen that somewhere in her father's missal. That was Christmas, the lights shining in the darkness, bringing hope and cheer.

"I love Christmas," said Tess.

"You say that every Christmas," her mother said tolerantly. "Your new bonnet is very festive. That shade of deep red suits you, but don't wear lighter reds. Christmas is nice for children and young people, but there's a lot of work and nothing much to it besides. Much ado about nothing, is what I say."

Tess sighed to herself. The account of the birth of Jesus in St. Luke's Gospel was among her favourite passages in Gwen's bible. And in her father's missal, she'd found many beautiful prayers and hymns celebrating that blessed night when Jesus was born, poor and humble, in a stable in Bethlehem. She longed to attend Midnight Mass. The candles, the singing, the incense, the atmosphere of heavenly peace and joy that must attend there…Her memories stirred as she strove to remember her father. Was he still with them? Or had he ceased to exist?

She had heeded Jesus' exhortations to pray, and she prayed often. The Lord's Prayer was her favourite.

"It's all true, you know," she said to her mother.

"Oh no, you only feel like that because of the sentimental memories of your father. He was a good man, though. I wonder if we'd have been happy if he'd lived. We were very different."

The carriage jogged on, leaving the lights and carols behind them.

"I was very hard on you, Tess. I had to be, for you to make something of yourself. I hope you don't hold it against me. You see now how your education helps in the business, the accounts and all that you keep for me, not to mention reading the new printed patterns that are getting fashionable, I'd never have managed this without you."

Tess' eyes filled with tears. She wanted to embrace her mother. True, they didn't see eye to eye about many things, but a mother's love was a blessing. Perhaps an important part of loving somebody was trying to understand them.

"We're here," said her mother. "That was very timely. We'll be in and out before we know it, and settle down to a warm supper."

CHAPTER 23

THEFT

Stella was on tenterhooks until she heard the knock on the back door. She opened it to admit her brother Eddie.

"Have you got them? Are you sure nobody saw you?"

"I'm sure. I slipped in and got them when they were all at lunch and I wasn't needed by anybody, for Browne was only required to serve."

"They won't miss them? Before tonight, I mean?"

"Oh no, nobody ever looks at that silver set. Like I told you, it's kept in a cupboard in the narrow hallway leading to the sewing room."

"It's beautiful," Stella said, taking up the silver teapot, the jug, and sugar bowl in turn. "What, do you 'ave something else?" Her brother was digging deep into his inside pocket.

"Jewellery," he grinned. "I had a bit of luck there. I 'ad to go to Mrs. Baddelley's room to help move a new chest of drawers, and Browne left me alone to go and get some more 'elp. It was that heavy, it was. I opened a drawer, rummaged in the back, and found this." He held up a necklace. Stella almost screamed as she took it in her hands.

"Diamonds, Eddie! Diamonds! They'll miss them right away, afore she even leaves the house, and it won't work!"

"Stella, you 'ave to trust my intelligence. It won't be missed. Anyway, it was in a box, a black velvet box. That's still there."

"Are you sure it won't be missed?"

"If it was, there'd 'ave been a hue and cry afore now. Look, I 'ave to go. Culpeper will miss me soon. I told 'im I had to see you to give you a Christmas present. He didn't like it, but let me go. If I'm noticed coming and going from here, that would be the explanation. Oh, blimey! I forgot it!"

"Never mind my present. Go, go! I'm terrified now!" Stella almost screamed at him and pushed him out the door.

"Hide that stuff," said her brother, indicating the silver and the diamonds.

"Of course, I will! I won't be easy until it's in the pillowcase and the police have it! Oh, by the way, I took some purple silk from there to make Aunt a Christmas present. I want to work on it now, so go away."

Stella stood in the middle of the living room floor with the necklace in her hands. The candles made the gems sparkle and gleam, and she was so nervous that they seemed to burn her fingers. Why had Eddie done such a foolish thing? The silver would have been enough to put her away for a while! But this? What if Mrs. Woods could prove that she had never been up to Mrs. Baddelley's bedchamber? Had she ever been upstairs? Did she know the house?

She was terrified. How much was this worth? But as time went on, her terror gave way to something else, greed. This might not be missed for weeks. Why worry about it now? After Mrs. Woods was arrested, she was to go back to Aunt Myrtle, and she'd take it with her. Aunt Myrtle would know what to do with it. In the meantime, she'd hide it somewhere safe. There was a loose floorboard in her room; it could be hidden there.

Eddie made his way back up to Baddelley Hall and saw Mrs. Woods and her daughter in a hansom, pulling out of the gate.

"You were gone too long," said Mr. Culpeper frostily when he got in. "Go and help put up the decorations in the front hall."

"I need to 'ave a private word with you, Mr. Culpeper, if you don't mind."

CHAPTER 24

FRAMED

After speaking with the butler, Eddie made his way up to the housekeeper's apartments.

"Mrs. Henley, I wonder if I might 'ave a word with you? It's a delicate matter." He stood humbly before the housekeeper.

"What is it, Dobbs? Can't it wait?"

"I don't think it can, Ma'am. It involves theft, you see."

Now Mrs. Henley was all ears. She put down the box of decorations.

"Theft! Tell me," she said, all ears.

"It's my sister, Stella, Mrs. Henly. She's in service to Mrs. Woods, the dressmaker."

"Well, yes, what is wrong with Stella?"

"She's very upset. She sees Mrs. Woods put away a lot of fine stuffs for herself. She's frightened to say anything. Most of the stuff comes from this house."

"Is she sure?"

"She's certain, Madam."

"Very well, I shall have a word with Mrs. Baddelley tomorrow morning."

"It's not just fabrics, Mrs. Henley. It's things from the house. This house." Eddie drew in his breath. "A silver teapot. She boasted to my sister that she lifted it from the cupboard in the back 'allway, and before I came to you, I told Mr. Culpeper and he checked. He's lookin' about to see if anything else is missing, and he said to come to you about it."

Mrs. Henly frowned. This was worrisome, and at Christmas too! Mrs. Baddelley would not want to deal with a thief in the middle of the festive season, and with so much upon her mind with her son's marriage to Lady Antonia, but it had to be done. She dismissed Eddie, thanked him, and with a big sigh, she set off for the drawing room, where she asked Mrs. Baddelley for a private word.

Mrs. Baddelley looked stricken when she told her in the hall. She sat down in shock. Mr. Culpeper arrived. As far as he could tell, nothing else was missing besides the silver.

Mr. Baddelley had to be informed, and he insisted that a message be sent immediately to the police. Mrs. Woods might be a 'fence' he said, and she'd get rid of the stuff by the morning. Who knows how long she had the silver already?

"What of my expensive materials from London?" Mrs. Baddelley was becoming agitated. "I had no idea she was a thief! I didn't miss anything!"

Mr. Baddelley was already giving orders to Mr. Culpeper to send for the police.

CHAPTER 25

THE ARREST

"We 'ad a long day. Time to turn in." Mrs. Woods yawned after the supper of soup, warmed bread, and crumbly white cheese. "Cover the fire, Tess, so there'll be a glowing coal or two in the morning."

"May I turn in for the night, Mrs. Woods?" Stella asked. She seemed nervous.

"Yes, of course. Are you all right, Stella?"

"Oh yes, Ma'am. Just a bit tired, if the truth be told."

"You can 'ave Boxing Day off. We'll do for ourselves."

"Thank you, Ma'am." Stella curtsied and went to her little room at the top the staircase. There, she sat on the bed, her heart beating so fast she thought she might die. The necklace was under the floorboard. Was it safe enough there? Perhaps Eddie was right, and she should have put it in the pillowcase too! If she were caught with it…

She heard voices from the street outside, and a very loud rap at the door. She jumped into bed fully dressed and covered her head.

Downstairs, Mrs. Woods was putting out the candles. The loud rap and the call *'Police! Open up!'* startled her. Tess was in her nightgown with her hair down around her shoulders. She pulled on her dressing gown.

"What on earth can you want in here?" she heard her mother ask as the men's boots were heard in the room adjoining.

"We want to search your premises, Mrs. Woods."

Tess immediately thought of the pillowcase with the remnants. Surely they were not after those little bits and pieces at this time of night? Should she go to the wardrobe and move it? But before she could make up her mind, the door opened, and a constable stood there.

"Out to the front room," he ordered her. She gathered her gown tightly around her and slipped past him, joining her mother, who was sitting nervously at one of the tables in the workroom.

"What is this about?" her mother asked the police matron, who had accompanied the constables. The matron did not reply, but Tess was frightened. Why did they send a woman, only to search and perhaps accompany a woman to the police station?

The landlord, Mr. Nicholls, came downstairs, looking like thunder.

"What is this about?" he barked, holding the candle crookedly in his hand, peering out from under his nightcap.

"I don't know, Mr. Nicholls, truly I don't!" Mrs. Woods wept.

"I think I have something here!" they heard, and the first constable brought the pillowcase out to the sewing table and turned it upside down.

"They're only remnants," Mrs. Woods protested. "The perks of my work! Perquisites! Like the cooks are allowed to keep fat from the roast, I'm allowed to keep those useless bits of material. Surely there's nothing criminal about that?"

"Mama, Mama!" Tess clutched her elbow. For among the piles of organdie and satin pouring out on the table, some objects clinked and sparkled in the torchlight.

"Who owns those?" Mrs. Woods was astonished. "How did they get there?"

"I'm placing you under arrest for theft, Mrs. Woods," said the constable. "And what's the girl's name?"

"She's Teresa Mary Woods."

"She's under arrest too."

"Thieves! I'm harbouring thieves!" Mr. Nicholls' nightcap appeared to dance on his head, so vigourously did he express himself. "That's not to be borne! Ye'll never come back 'ere to this house, never! Ye brought the police on me. Such a thing never 'appened before!" He continued to shout as the police brought the women roughly to their feet.

Tess could not believe this was happening. It was like a horrid dream.

"You may get dressed," said the constable, and nodded to the matron, who ushered them into the bedroom and watched every move as they put on their undergarments, petticoats, stockings, and wool gowns. Mother and daughter's fingers trembled so much they could hardly do each other's buttons, hooks, and eyes. She searched their pockets and nodded to them to get their outerwear and to put on their boots. When Mrs. Woods reached for her reticule, she took it from her.

As they were being led out, Tess saw Stella on the staircase. She was still fully dressed. The candle she held lit her face in the darkness with an eerie glow. She wore a strange expression, no surprise, no distress. There was a kind of pleasure in her eyes. How could it be? How could she enjoy what was happening to them? Tess nudged her mother to look up. Mother and daughter exchanged a glance.

Both knew then how the silver had gotten into the pillowcase. But why? What had Stella got against them?

CHAPTER 26

IN JAIL

They were hustled into the police van, and they set off. It was late, very cold, and foggy. Mother and daughter were trembling.

"Mama, what's going to happen to us?" Tess whispered. The matron looked at her and frowned.

"No talking," she commanded.

The carol singers were still out in full force, accompanied by flutes and trumpets, almost like a marching band.

Deck the halls with boughs of holly, falalalalalala!

Tis the season to be jolly, falalalalalala!

It seemed like a mockery.

Tess put her hand up to her bonnet, and without thinking, scratched it on the sprig of holly. She ought to tear it out and throw it on the floor. There was no festivity to be had now!

At the drab and cold police station they were separated and put into different cells. Tess found herself with other women who were sleeping and did not welcome the disruption. In the dim light of the matron's lamp, she could not see how many there were. There was a strong smell of whiskey or beer. The matron motioned her toward an empty bunk, and she lay down on coarse straw, shivering, trying not to cry loudly because of the other people. All was dark. She felt herself being bitten all over and got up to try to shake the vermin off herself.

Where was Mama? Tears rolled down her cheeks unchecked. Why had they not allowed them to be together?

The following morning, the other women woke up, yawned, and picked parasites off each other. They went in turn to the bucket in the corner to relieve themselves. They took no notice of Tess at first, until there was more light in the cell, and they could see that she was terrified.

"First time in 'ere, eh?" said a coarse-looking redhead, staring at her. "You'll get used to it. Where did you get picked up?"

"At my home," stammered Tess.

"Home? They went there for you? Do you entertain at 'ome, then?" said another.

"Shut up, Marge, she's not like one of us. Can't you see she's respectable?"

"Oh." Then – "What are you in for? What's your name?"

"Teresa Woods. My mother and I were arrested wrongly for theft. We were set up. I don't know where she is. They separated us."

"So you won't get a chance to make your stories agree," said the redhead. "They call it '*corroboration*'.

The other girls laughed.

"Obviously, you've *corroborated*," said an older girl. She had several teeth missing when she laughed, but her lips were scarlet from carmine, and a smell of beer came from her clothes.

"Why are you in here?" Tess asked timidly.

There was silence.

"Why are we in 'ere? Answer the young miss," said Marge.

"We're of the night, no better than we should be," Angie said. She was the one with the red hair.

There was a commotion at the door, a slot opened, and four bowls were handed in one after another, and four rolls of black bread.

Tess looked at the food in the bowl. It was a thin porridge without milk. Dark specks floated on top. It was impossible to know what they were or what they had been.

"Ye better eat it. Ye'll get nothing else till evening," urged Peg, her mouth full of bread.

She took her spoon and ate. It was warm. The bread was horrible, but she ate that too.

The prison door swung open, and her name was called. At last! She and her Mama would be reunited and sent home.

Instead, the warden handed her over to a constable, who led her to a small room in which a hatless policeman sat at a table, a book in front of him.

"Now Miss Woods,– suppose you tell me how that silver came to be at your house. Don't lie, I always know if a suspect lies."

"The servant put it there!" cried Tess.

"Now why would she do that?"

"To get us into trouble – I don't know."

"What? Did you not get on well?"

"No. I mean, we did. I thought she was nice, but when I saw her on the stairs, I knew it was her. Please, sir, can I see my mother?"

To her great relief, a meeting was allowed later that day. She and her mother met in another small room with a warden in attendance.

Mrs. Woods looked haggard, tired, and worried.

"Tess, they're going to release you tomorrow," she said. "You're to go to Cumberland to the Stowes."

"But aren't they going to release you too, Mama?"

"Not yet. To be found in possession of stolen goods is a bad thing. We know who put it there. I've told 'em."

"So, are they going to arrest her?"

"I doubt it very much." Mrs. Woods eyes dropped to the floor.

"Why would Stella do such a thing, Mama? How have we ever 'urt her?"

"We haven't."

"Another minute!" rapped the warden.

"Tess, I want to tell you quickly.– Go to Mrs. Hanks and tell her that I need counsel. Her son is an attorney. Do you remember where she lives?"

Mrs. Hanks was a regular client. Tess knew where she lived,– Avenham Lane. She had taken work there.

"Ask Mrs. Hanks to arrange for you to go to Cumberland. She's a good woman, and she'll look after you."

"I won't go to Cumberland, Mama."

Her mother looked very impatient, and she got that look that Tess knew she had to obey.

"You will go to the Stowes! They're your guardians! Don't have me worryin' about you out on the streets. You heard Mr. Nicholl! You're 'omeless!"

"Time's up," said the matron smoothly.

"Mama!" cried Tess, with pain in her voice. She hated her mother to be angry with her, and she didn't want to part like this! She made a rush toward her to embrace her, but the warden stopped her.

Mrs. Woods' expression softened a little.

"When they let me go, I'll come to fetch you," she said. The warden pushed her mother from the room and slammed the door.

That night, the carol singers sang outside the prison. She had to listen to 'Deck the Halls' again, trumpets, drums, and all. She covered her ears.

CHAPTER 27

BACK TO MEADOW ST

Tess was released the following morning. She had nothing with her, and though she begged to see her mother again, she was not allowed.

When the door shut behind her, she found herself alone on the cold, drab street, the high wall of the prison, which ran its length, towering over her. The fog had not lifted, and there was a malevolence in the chill of the day. She felt so small, so alone. She had to go to Avenham, but first, she needed to go home.

She headed toward Meadow Street at a run. As she approached her home, for she had not ceased to think of it as such, she saw a pile of objects against the wall of the house. What could it be? When she got closer, she saw that it was a small heap of her mother's belongings, and her own also. Upset, she peered in the window. The front room was as bare as it had been on the day they had moved in, with just the furniture and curtains.

"What are you doing?" The harsh voice of Mr. Nicholls burst upon her like a gun in her ear. She whirled about. "Didn't I tell you never to darken my doorstep again? Did I not make myself clear?"

Tess pointed down to the pile of things by the wall, sodden with the rain.

"I took all of your belongings out here," he said. "I kept a few things because you owed me a week's rent."

Tess became aware that a neighbour had emerged from next door – Mrs. Campbell was a good, righteous woman, and she wondered if she, too, despised the Woods now.

"Take them and get out. Don't ever let me see you in this street again, you or your criminal mother," he snarled, whacking the pathetic pile of belongings with his cane. He took his key from his waistcoat pocket, unlocked the door, and let himself in.

Tess rummaged hopelessly in the pathetic pile at her feet. They were only older clothes and things too threadbare to wear anymore. Mrs. Campbell approached.

"Tess, you poor dear, what a horrid thing to happen!"

"Where's everything else?" Tess indicated the pile. "Where are all our clothes?"

"Stolen, I'm afraid, the very day he put them out. No doubt he kept some nice things for his own daughters."

"We have nothing!"

"I found a book of Roman prayers and brought it inside. It was a little damaged from damp, but not much."

"Father's missal!" Tess felt very grateful. Had she lost that, she would have been inconsolable.

Mrs. Campbell brought her inside her home and asked about her mother over a cup of tea and Christmas cake. Tess stared at the cake numbly. She had forgotten it was Christmas – Eve!

Then she remembered her duty. She had to go to Avenham Lane without delay. She jumped up, said a quick good bye to the surprised Mrs. Campbell, and ran all the way to Avenham Lane.

CHAPTER 28

HOMELESS

Tess ran to Avenham Lane. She knew the house, – a red brick building with bay windows behind a small and neat lawn. She let herself in the gate and went around the back, knocking on the servant's entrance. She did not even notice that her hair hung in wet streaks around her face and that her navy cloak was stained with mud, and her red bonnet was dripping. The holly was bedraggled, the berries gone, making a mockery of it.

It was opened by a cross cook. "Who are you? What do you want? We're very busy today."

"I have to see Mrs. Hanks. It's very important. –You see my mother was arrested! – It's all a big mistake. –She sent me here –"

Tess was not practiced enough to be able to couch her request in such a way as to get on the good side of whom she was speaking to. She came across to the cook as a bedraggled wretch whose mother was a criminal, and so she shut the door. Tess cried out in despair and ran to the front door. Perhaps the butler or the housekeeper would be kinder.

The experience had taught her very quickly that perhaps her approach was not the best. She tried to calm herself. She prayed the Lord's Prayer while waiting on the doorstep.

The butler answered, and taking her for a beggar, told her to go around the back, but she said quickly. "I'm sorry, sir." That would make him feel good. "They're very busy and won't see me. I would be obliged if you could get Mrs. Hanks. I need to speak to her about an urgent matter. Please, could she spare me a moment?"

Had she really said it so well? The butler's expression softened. He saw a young girl who had got the worst of the weather and who was in need. Unfortunately, he could not help her.

"I'm sorry, Miss. Mrs. Hanks was taken ill last November. She is abed and cannot speak."

"It's her son, the attorney. My mother needs his services. She has an urgent need."

"Mr. Hanks will not be here for Christmas. His wife is, er, confined. I'm sorry."

He shut the door.

Tess was now in a great turmoil. She had nowhere to turn, except to go back to Meadow Street, the only place where she knew people, and put herself under the protection of one of her neighbours there, and hope that one of the men, perhaps Mr. Campbell, would know how to proceed. She trudged back, only to find that when she reached the section where her home was, she was met by a hail of stones by a group of youths and girls, people she knew! Two of the youths ran towards her and caught her, attempting to drag her down a laneway, but her screams made them let her go. She began to run until she did not know where she was.

Mrs. Boyce! If she could find her way out of this warren of laneways and alleys at the back of a large hulking mill she did not recognise, she'd go to Mrs. Boyce and seek shelter in her cottage. But the longer she walked, the more lost she became. She had no idea where she was, and she felt an overpowering hunger. The prison gruel and unwholesome bread had not filled her for even an hour. She had raced away from Mrs. Campbell's hospitality. Now what was she to do? Worst of all, she had done nothing for her mother.

The day became evening. Even in the dark, damp, stinking, and muddy neighbourhood lights went up and people looked merry. They were merry, for there were taverns and public houses galore, and laughter and merriment within. The narrow crooked streets were filling up with people, and some spoke in a strange language. Then she heard carol singing somewhere. Happy singing. She felt mocked. People were happy, she thought, and she and her mother were utterly miserable, because in the space of one day, they had lost their home, their possessions, and their good name, and it could get worse for both if there was not a miracle.

As long as she lived, she would never forget this Christmas, she thought, as she seated herself on an upturned crate left alongside the wall of a shop shut for the evening. She smelled food cooking, but she had no money. After a few moments, she was asleep.

CHAPTER 29

CHRISTMAS

"Ah come on now, Miss! Wake up, and sure we'll 'ave a bit of fun!"

The breath in her face smelled of whiskey, and she felt a hand upon her calf, groping under her skirt. She jumped up, almost knocking the man over. A string of curses in a foreign language followed her as she sped away.

It must be very late! The taverns had emptied, and swaying figures made their way along the pavements. To avoid them, she slipped into a laneway dimly lit by a gas lamp and stood against the wall. She could barely make out the hovels along the lane, but in every one, a candle was lit in the front window.

Church bells began to ring, pealing joyously upon the night air.

Of course, it was Christmas. What was Christmas? St Luke wrote a detailed account of it, the account she had always loved to read, but in secret, because her mother disapproved, calling religion nonsense.

Her mother was right! It must be! What kind of joy was there for her or for her mother tonight? Cold, hard reality was all that was hers.

Then the lights in most of the windows began to be extinguished. One by one they quickly went out.

Suddenly, the doors around her opened and people poured out on the street. Old women wrapped head to heel in shawls, old men with caps and hats, younger people in cloaks. The sounds of boots and clogs crunching along was like a disorganized quick march. Entire families walked past her on their way to Midnight Mass. Nobody noticed her. The trooping lasted all of five minutes, they all turned around the same corner, and the laneway was deserted again. She felt desolate, alone and cast aside. God, if there was a God, had cast her aside.

Her eyes were drawn to the few lights left in the windows, flickering in steady flames. And as she gazed on one window, she saw the shape of an old woman tend the candle.

It came upon her that she could knock upon the door. What harm would it do? And she might just ask for a bite to eat, just enough to keep her strength up. The more she thought about it, the more she was convinced she should try, so she made her way over to the house and knocked timidly on the door. It creaked open, and a grey head poked out.

"Yes?"

"Excuse me. I'm lost and..." Her voice trailed away, but her broken appearance spoke for her.

The old woman appeared to hesitate a moment, before she said, "Come in, you poor craythur."

CHAPTER 30

THE RYANS

She was Mrs. Ryan, and she had stayed at home 'to mind the baby' who was sleeping in a crib in the corner. She put Tess sitting down at the table and set two boiled potatoes in front of her, as well as a sausage, a strip of fried bacon, and a cup of milk.

"I have no money to pay you." Tess burst into tears.

"I don't want to be paid, Miss. If I can't give a *craythur* a bit to eat at Christmas, when the Holy Family is looking for a place to stop and rest, then I'm not a good Christian. What's your name, *craythur*?"

"Teresa Woods. Tess."

"Miss Tess, how came you to this? Where are your mother and father?"

Tess poured out her story. Mrs. Ryan listened, and then said she had to stay the night, because she could not go back out into the streets. She bade her lie on a couch and covered her with a blanket. Tess did not even hear her son and daughter-in-law return from Mass, nor did she hear Mrs. Ryan's explanation of the strange girl asleep on the couch. She did not hear Denis Ryan's mild reproach to his mother for taking in a complete stranger, nor hear the baby cry and his wife Kate soothe him, nor did the aroma of the Christmas breakfast, breaking their meatless Advent fast, awaken her. Tess slept until the afternoon, and when she woke did not know where she was for several moments.

She was bidden to take part in a simple Christmas dinner, roast flesh of some kind. She could not tell and did not like to ask. The meat was served with potatoes and brussels sprouts, followed by a quarter of an orange each, which was a great wonder and a treat to the young couple. Mrs. Ryan had hidden it for days before it was triumphantly brought to the table. She laughed when Denis asked her where she had got it. And there was Christmas cake, strong dark fruit cake. It had been a long time ago when she first heard of Christmas cake. She wondered how her mother was spending Christmas Day, and she felt miserable, though she smiled in order to be grateful and polite.

Denis thought he knew somebody who could help her. Father Graves? Would she object to taking advice from a Catholic priest?

"Oh no," she said. "I am Catholic. I was baptised."

This seemed to promise that the way forward would be even more smooth, and the following day, after another night on the couch, Denis took her to see Father Graves.

The priest was amazed she had not received any instruction in her faith, nor had made her Communion or Confirmation, and keenly wished to remedy that, more than helping her to find an attorney for her mother. However, Denis gently prodded him back to the object of the visit, and he gave her the name of a Mr. Higgins.

"I will go and see him tomorrow," she said to Denis as they walked back to the little cottage in Mill Row. "But how am I to repay you for your kindness?"

Denis mumbled that there was no need, that it was Christmas, but Tess had already seen that there was a great deal of cleaning and mending to be done at their cottage. Mrs. Ryan had arthritic fingers, and Kate had no time because of working at the mill and tending the baby when she was at home. But how poor their clothes were! The coarsest cottons and worsted, much of it threadbare. It was nothing at all like she was used to working with, but she mended and patched as if it was of great value, as it was to this poor family. Best of all, the family did not seem to think it strange that her mother had been unjustly imprisoned, and they were very ready to believe she had been falsely accused. Tess caught the impression that perhaps it had either happened to them at some time in the past, or to somebody they knew.

They knew, for instance, that you could only visit the prison on Saturdays, so it was with joy and relief that Tess and her mother met again the Saturday before the New Year.

"Where are you staying?" was the first question her mother asked. "Did Mrs. Campbell take you in?"

Tess told her what had happened and how she had ended up with the Ryans.

"With Irish!" Her mother was astounded. She had never thought much of the Irish.

"Yes, Mama, and they're very kind. I'm going to get a job at the mill -"

"Oh, no, you are not." Her mother had that look in her eye again. "You're to write to Aunt Belle to come from Cumberland to collect you. You will go and live with them until I'm released. The trial won't take place until the spring court. I have to stay here until then," she sighed. "And it's worse than I thought. They're saying I took a diamond necklace, too. They're saying I was a 'fence', that I stole it from Mrs. Baddelley's bedchamber and got rid of it immediately, that I gave it to some criminals, because it's not to be found anywhere. I was never in her bedchamber! I don't even know where it was! They say I followed a maid up there or something, and slipped in and took this necklace, worth over two hundred pounds!"

Tess was distraught to hear this. "But Mama, I got counsel for you," she said proudly.

"Mr. Hanks! He has not been in touch with me yet." Her mother sounded vexed.

"Oh no, Mother." Tess told her it was a Mr. Higgins, and her mother became very agitated.

"What else can I do, Mama?" Tess sounded despairing. There was silence. Her mother sighed.

Tess took an apple out of her cloak pocket. The warden nodded, and she handed it to her mother.

"Where did you get it?" her mother asked.

"The Ryans gave it to me," she lied. She had stolen it from a fruit stall on her way to the jail. She was not happy about stealing, but she had to have a gift for her mother, and she had no money. She had another one concealed deep in her pocket for the Ryans. Her mother gave her a long look, and Tess knew that she knew she had stolen them. Why should she be worried, after all the remnants she had taken?

"You mustn't stay with those Ryans any longer," her mother said then. "Go and stay with the Campbells. They're respectable people in a respectable area."

Tess wanted to tell her about the reception she had received from Meadow Street but she held her tongue.

"Don't forget to write to Aunt Belle."

"All right, Mama." Tess knew when she had to obey. She wondered where she would get pen and paper, but Denis would come to her aid again. They and their neighbours seemed to share everything. What one lacked, another would provide.

"Time's up," said the warden.

"Mama," she said eagerly before they parted. "I feel the same way as you do now about faith. I don't believe either."

To her great surprise, her mother's reaction was not one of approval.

"Teresa Woods," she scolded, "I have done nothing else except pray since I got in 'ere. You are not to give it up."

"But, Mama," Teresa said in great astonishment. "You never pray!"

"I do now. I find it good. Remember to write to Aunt Belle."

It was a tearful farewell. Mrs. Woods told her to be a good girl, and not to allow any boy to take any liberties with her until she was married, nothing beyond a kiss.

"Mama, you'll be out in the spring! I'm not going to marry for years!"

"Just in case it goes against me, love."

Her mother rarely called her by an endearment. Tears shone in the older woman's eyes. After Tess had left, she shed them freely. She felt it would not go well for her.

The following day, she bid goodbye to the Ryans and set out for Meadow Street, hoping that her reception would be kinder there. Christmas had come and gone, people had more or less forgotten already, and she reached Campbells without being set upon or even noticed. They took her in.

CHAPTER 31

BELLE AND JIM CUMBERLAND

Jim Stowe had a public house in the village of Stagtarn, with a few rooms above the premises for lodging travellers, and above that, a bedroom and a living room where he and his wife lived. Above that were two attic rooms. Their servant Annie inhabited one of them, and the other lay empty,

They heard the gossip of all the area, and in the little village not yet reached by the railway, they depended upon each other to make news. Mrs. Stowe did not go downstairs at night, unless there were women in the snuggery, so she relied upon her husband for news when he came upstairs.

"Who was in tonight?" she asked early one morning after he had come upstairs to bed. He had come to expect to be quizzed, as she wanted all the news. She was sitting up in bed, her nightcap on over her curlers, and a warm plaid shawl about her shoulders.

"Oooh, let's see now. Stone and his cousin Farley. He was grumbling that Farley means to stop with him for the whole winter, and he talks about his last job all the time, Stone and his missus are sick of it. Then there was Joe Pepper, and he said to tell you that his wife was delivered of a little boy, or was it a girl? I can't rightly remember."

"You can't remember?" she said, annoyed. "It's not a hard thing to remember. But I'll find out tomorrow. Is Mrs. Pepper well?"

"He'd 'ave said if she wasn't, and he'd not 'ave come out," was her husband's feeble reply, to which she snorted.

"Tim Pepper would come out for a beer if all belonging to him had died that very day. Anybody else?"

He disliked this nightly interrogation, but it was her usual way.

"There was Reggie Turnbull, bragging as usual about his fine connections."

"Ah, you mean with Mrs. Bailey?" Belle's blue eyes were brightened in her round pink face.

"Yes, and implying it was more than it is. He claims she's in love with him."

"Why does a gentrified woman like Mrs. Bailey stop there and leave herself open to that talk?"

"They are two schemers."

Belle laughed.

"They can scheme all they want, but the estate will not have Livingstone blood again. Mr. Alexander cheated 'em, din't he? He has no intention of dying, but if he ever meets with an accident on a dark night, we'll all know what happened."

"The world will know it," said Jim, climbing into bed.

"Perhaps," Belle said craftily, "perhaps the next time Mr. Alexander gives his horse to Turnbull while he takes a stroll around the village, he'll put a pebble under the saddle, and be handsomely paid for it." She laughed and poked him with her elbow.

They settled down to sleep on this cold night, unaware that the morning would bring very alarming news.

Their post was delivered to the public house around ten o'clock. There was a demand for nine pounds, four shillings, and sixpence from a tradesman in Penrith, a letter of apology from a Mr. Greene Jim had banned from his pub for breaking a chair, and a letter addressed to Mrs.

Stowe in a familiar hand, that of Tess Woods. Annie brought it upstairs.

"She don't usually write after Christmas," said Belle, frowning as she tore it open. "We had a letter from 'er before. I hope nothing is wrong. Oh, oh, Mr. Stowe! Mr. Stowe! Tell him to come to me quick, Annie!"

When Jim ran upstairs, he found Belle sprawled back into a chair, the letter on her lap, her feet stuck out before her, screaming. Annie immediately got a box of snuff and rushed to her mistress' side.

"Elizabeth has been arrested! Oh, my own sister! She'll be hung!"

"What, was it murder? Did she kill that horrible woman then?" But Belle continued to scream, so he took up the letter.

"It's not as bad as you thought, Mrs. Stowe. Pull yourself together. She is sure she'll be acquitted come spring. Did you read the last part?"

"No, no, how could I, when I was thinking of Elizabeth swinging outside the jail, and crowds about cheering!"

"Tess is to come to us."

Mrs. Stowe recovered and sat up straight, pushing Annie and her snuff box away.

"What, Tess? That lass? I don't know if I'll want her about. She writes so proper, for one thing. I'm sure she will be very proper, and that's not us, Mr. Stowe."

"We are to go and fetch her here, she says."

"Well, the nerve! Oh, but poor Elizabeth! Elizabeth's not a thief! She's annoying and spoiled, but she's not a thief. A set of silver plate and a diamond necklace indeed! This must have been a set-up. It was that devil woman she wrote us about, she 'ad it in for her. Miss Devil. What if she's not acquitted, Jim, are we stuck with her?"

"Who?"

"Teresa! Who else?"

"Oh, I don't know. We'll apprentice her out somewhere."

"My poor little sister Elizabeth!" Belle's handkerchief was to her eyes.

"I never thought you were that much fond of Elizabeth," observed Jim. "And theft isn't a hangin' offense anymore."

"Of course, I am fond of her!"

Belle was the much older half-sister of Elizabeth. She had left home and gone into service by the time Elizabeth had been born, and on her rare visits to her home, she resented how her father doted on the baby, and as the years went by, how he taught her the trade. Why could she not have stayed at home and learned tailoring? She reflected that her parents wanted to be rid of the responsibility of feeding and clothing her.

Because she had a good mistress, Belle had been taught to read and write, but she still saw herself as hard done by. Sent out from her home to strangers at twelve, she saw her sister as replacing her, more coddled than she ever was, and then when Elizabeth was seventeen, she ran off with Michael Woods, the Catholic whose mother was from some dark-skinned country, Malta or somewhere like that.

"Jim, Tess can sew. If she can sew half as well as her mother, she'll earn her keep here."

"Who 'as to pay for Elizabeth's lawyers?"

"Oh, I don't know."

"She'll expect us to pony up."

"We won't."

"But if we don't, Belle, she might get bad advice and be locked up for years. And we're stuck with the girl. Girls are such an expense, too. Gowns and trinkets. What do you think? Should we offer to pay for the attorney?"

"We can offer a loan. Make it clear it's a loan, too."

"We'd better travel down and get the girl soon."

"Next week will be time enough, Jim. We shall put her in the attic. Annie, get that room aired. I know there's a mouse there. I hear it scratchin' above my head every night."

"Yes, ma'am." Annie was very surprised that 'Angela's room' would not be given to Miss Tess. Their daughter Angela was married in Dumfries and rarely came to see her parents.

"I expect Tess will have a lot of nice things to bring here, Jim. Her mother was doing well."

CHAPTER 32

STAGTARN

It had been a tiresome journey, and with every mile put between her and her mother in jail, Tess' heart grew heavier. She had no interest in looking out the window. Opposite her, Uncle Jim read a newspaper. He was gruff, and he had been very surprised that she only had one small poor bundle of belongings, which lay now at her feet. Everything in it had been given to her in charity by the Campbells or other neighbours who, now sorry for her, had provided her with a few hand-me-downs.

There was a muddy slush most of the way before they reached Stagtarn. The carriage wheels got stuck, and they had to disembark several times while the coachmen pushed and heaved them out. Tess was freezing. Uncle Jim had decided that his charge was sulking, and he cursed that they'd have to put up with her. She was a tall, scrawny figure in her navy cloak and red bonnet, and he wondered how he was going to stand her around his house for two or three months. Heaven forbid it would be longer!

Tess alighted the carriage onto a slushy street and almost at once collided with a man going into the public house.

"Sorry, Miss." He looked at her curiously, and then saw Jim Stowe getting out of the carriage after her.

"Eh, who's this Jim, your niece, is it?"

“My wife’s niece,” he replied shortly, as if to squash any idea that she was related to him.

“Didn’t know she ‘ad one,” said the man, and went inside.

“Come around the back,” said Jim to her. “We ‘ave our own entrance.”

A dark smelly alley, and she was conscious of male shapes skulking about.

“Don’t look,” was her uncle’s command. “Just don’t come out ‘ere at night. You’ll see things you’re not supposed to see.”

They walked up a dark, narrow staircase and he called out, “We’re ‘ere!”

. . .

The room she came into was large, and a warm fire was burning. Her aunt got up from her chair to welcome her. The table in the corner was set for supper.

Belle's welcome was warm, and she felt a little reassured. Her cloak and hat were taken and hung upon a peg by Annie.

"Where's the rest of your luggage? Is it being sent tomorrow?" Belle asked.

"That's all she has," Jim informed her in a surprised tone.

"Where are all your mother's belongings then?" Belle asked Tess. "I know she was getting nice things with her dressmaking for the gentry. Did you sell them? I suppose if you did, it's no harm, for now you'll be able to help with your keep."

The day had been very long for Tess, she was many, many miles from her mother and everybody she knew, her uncle had been dour, and now Belle expected her to have either valuables or money.

She burst into a fit of weeping.

"Waterworks," her uncle muttered. "Annie, where is supper? I'm that 'ungry."

"Oh, come now, Tess, you mustn't weep and cry like that," Belle said, and there was an edge to her voice that Tess did not miss. "I'll take you to your room, and when you've composed yourself, you can come down."

Tess meekly followed her up a small flight of stairs to the small room in the eaves.

"We don't light a fire in this room," her aunt said as if in explanation of the dark, unwelcome grate that did not even have a pretty fire screen in front to hide it's gaping emptiness. "The chimney's bricked up."

"I'm sorry for weeping," Tess said in a choking voice.

"You 'ave your troubles, but you have to deal with them, I was out in service in a strange house when I was twelve years old. Only twelve! How do you think I felt?"

This made Tess feel even worse, but with a great effort she controlled her tears.

"I'll have Annie bring some water for you to wash your face, and the privy is out the back for the daytime, but there's a chamber pot under the bed, and when you're ready you come and have supper, and tell me all about the misfortunes of your poor mother."

Annie came up with water.

"Now, Miss Tess, don't fret. It's a strange place I daresay, but folks 'ere are good, decent people, and in good weather, there's nowhere like Stagtarn. It's that luvly, it is. People from miles around come to see our lakes an' fens an' crags, and there's that poet, who wrote about the daffodils, 'e was from these parts, an' there's not a prettier place in England when the sun shines, and we 'ave the best gingerbread all year round, the best in England. You'll soon settle in." Then she was gone, but her kindness was like a balm to Tess' hurting heart, though her accent was very strange to her ears, and she pronounced some words very oddly.

In the living room, Belle was grim-faced.

"I'm disappointed in what I see. She's as plain as plain can be. She doesn't take after our side! I never saw her father, but he must have been an ugly fellow. Did you see that sallow complexion? And her mood! Did you ever see the like? With her grandmother from that place near Italy, where they're all emotional. She's too old to carry on like that. Elizabeth indulged her! She won't be indulged in this house. I hope we are not going to have to put up with *moods*."

Her husband grunted. His mouth was full of bread, and he slurped his soup.

"Why doesn't she have more possessions? I bet those Campbells took them. They stole them."

Annie, setting the supper down, listened with sadness in her heart for Miss Tess. She saw someone completely different, a poor lonely young girl, a lost soul. From the talk she overheard, Annie knew her mother was in prison, and she was very much to be pitied. Her employers were hard of heart, and she only stayed with them because there was no other work to be got year-round in Stagtarn.

The door opened and Tess came in, dry eyed, but with a puffy face and trembling hands. Belle sighed and sat by the fire, taking up her knitting, extending her stockinged feet to the fender to warm them. Annie got Tess settled and served her hot chicken soup, bread, and cheese.

CHAPTER 33

NEW FRIENDS

The following days were the worst Tess had ever known. Her aunt was cold and unfeeling, and her uncle ignored her. She entered into a place of loneliness in her heart and cried herself to sleep every night in her icy room with the bricked up chimney. Her heart was broken.

She wrote to her mother, hoping that it could be read to her. She put on a cheerful aspect in the letter, for there was no need to make her mother worry about her. She asked Jim for a stamp, and he grudgingly provided it. She longed for just a little money of her own, but they didn't offer her any.

From her first day, Tess was busy in the house. Her aunt had plenty for her to do. Hard work, she said, was best for people who were melancholy. She herself had learned the value of it, she reminded Tess very often, when she went into service at twelve years old, but she was well able to work before that, she added meaningfully, helping her mother from the time she could toddle, implying that Tess had led a life of laziness.

The days lengthened, the skies cleared a little, Tess was awakened by birdsong, and the little copse of trees opposite the tavern sported new, green buds. Her aunt rose very late because she went to bed late, and Tess had the living room to herself in the mornings. She found Annie's company comforting, even if they did not speak much, and she took the opportunity to go for walks after her breakfast, and as she often had a list of errands for her aunt, she took a basket and enjoyed leaving the house for a time.

She had to own that the village was pretty, but very quiet. It lay in a valley. The Stagtarn Arms, a tall, narrow building of grey slate, dominated one side of the village. The smallest school Tess had ever seen was perched on a hill, behind a wild patch of grass where flowers were coming up. Just beyond the school, a bridge led over a rushing stream. When she crossed the bridge, she was on the village's main street, but the houses were scattered with patches of green in between, or trees. The tradesmen's shops were here, and further on, a large smart-looking Inn, The Reginald. Attached was a large yard and stables.

The air was fresh, unlike the air she was used to in the city, but the wind was piercing.

As she walked along, she hoped that she would be liked here, although it was only a temporary stay.

Unknown to Tess, the Stowes were not popular in Stagtarn. Her uncle was a moneylender, and he had broken many families by his ruthless collection of outstanding loans with interest. Her aunt was known to never contribute toward any collection for charity. The leftover food for the lodgers was thrown out rather than given to the poor widows in the Almshouses. The villagers regarded this niece of theirs with wariness, but thanks to Annie Ware, they softened toward her, and pitied her having to stay with the Stowes. Before long, Tess was receiving friendly looks, and after that, as she exchanged words with the tradespeople and in the shops while waiting to be served, she was accepted for her own sake, and was regarded as a nice, well-mannered girl. Only the youths judged her not worth knowing because of her gawkiness and her spots, but as she was as yet not interested in boys, she didn't in the least mind that they ignored her, and was rather glad of it, because she hated to be noticed.

She made two friends, Jeanie and Mary, whose fathers were blacksmith and baker, respectively. They hailed her one day and asked if she would walk with them. After that, the three girls often went together around the village on their errands. Annie had been very discreet on her behalf, and nobody knew that her mother was in jail. Everybody assumed she was an orphan.

One day, as they walked up toward The Reginald, for Mary had to deliver some loaves there, they saw a youth on a fine horse riding toward them. He was tall, slim, and good-looking. Jeanie and Mary huddled together and giggled a bit. He took no notice and rode on.

"Who's that?" asked Tess.

"It's Master Bailey from Stagtarn Hall. Is he not very 'andsome?"

"I didn't really see his face," Tess said.

"No, you cannot in such a very short time as it took him to ride past." Jeanie said. "He often goes to the tarn and walks there. I came by him once quite by accident. I came around the side of a large rock, and there he was, coming in the opposite direction. He gave me a very civil nod of the 'ead."

"He swims in the tarn," Mary said.

"Yes, and he nearly died of an accident in Thora, but was saved. That lake is haunted, it is."

"Has he got brothers and sisters?"

"He has a stepbrother and three stepsisters. Their mother does not like him, because he will inherit everything," Jeanie said.

"My father said he was supposed to die young," Mary supplied. "But he didn't! Now my father says the younger brother will get nothing, but what's nothing to them is different to what's nothing to us! Oh, look! Look! There is the mother!"

They had turned in the gate of the inn, and there was a carriage in front of the door. A lady alighted. She was small and very elegant in a black velvet cloak with a fur lined hood and a fur muff. She looked about her a little furtively before she went in.

"I wonder what her business is there," mused Jeanie. Mary snorted and laughed. No more was said.

CHAPTER 34

TURNBULL

"Reggie, may I speak with you?" Mrs. Bailey sidled up to Reginald Turnbull's side, not that there was anybody around to see the closeness that accompanied her request.

He turned about to face her and took her hands in his, kissing her fingers through her gloves. She had set out to make him adore her, and he did. She did not love him, though he was handsome and well-made. Sometimes she was afraid he would ask her to run away with him, with Lily, so she deflected any expressions of eternal ardour if she could.

He led her into the warm parlour and seated her by the fire.

"What is your trouble?"

"You know it well!" She drew off her gloves and tossed her hood back. Her mouth pouted, her brow was spoiled by a frown, and flaxen curls without a trace of grey framed her face.

"You really have your heart set on it, don't you?"

"There is nothing else in the world I care about!" she snapped "He is approaching manhood, and Clarence, I have told, I always tell my son that everything will be his, and it will be!"

"I tried to help you. It didn't work. Can't you leave it be? It's dangerous work."

"No." Her tone was short. "If you love me, you'll try again. Then I'll be happy, very happy." She looked up at him and smiled a pretty smile. Her teeth were still very good.

"I have a little time this morning," she said, smiling her coy smile.

As he kissed her, Mr. Turnbull wondered if he was a fool, but at least Lydia was unaware of his resolution. He had no intention of making another attempt on Alexander's life. He had a child now, and someday she might need him.

CHAPTER 35

SENTENCING

Tess was overjoyed to see a letter addressed to her. Was it from her mother? Had she got someone to write? She had, and it was someone of education, for the hand was neat and every word spelled correctly.

Dear Tess, I received your letter. I am happy you are settled with Belle. Be of as much help to her as you can. I have no date for my trial yet. The lawyer went on my behalf to Baddelleys to ask them to drop the case, but they refused. Stella Hobbs has not been found. The diet here is what you expect. I am in good enough health. The lady writing for me is a good Christian woman who visits us. Her name is Mrs. Bright. She reads us the Bible sometimes. You will be surprised to hear that I like to hear it. Please pray for me. Kind regards to Belle and Jim. Love from your fond mother.

Tess was relieved to get a letter but frustrated to hear that no progress had been made on her mother's case.

Spring came in, and with it the quarterly trials that took place in every district. Her uncle told her of it.

"I would so like to attend my mother's trial," she pleaded, but her aunt and uncle would not hear of it. It was too far, and a courtroom was no place for a young girl.

"If it goes badly, she'll be too distraught, and I don't want to have the responsibility of looking after her," said Jim privately to his wife.

"And I can't go, because carriages upset my stomach something terrible," Belle said.

Jim took the paper daily, and he knew when the court was sitting. He scanned the names of the convicted every day. Then one evening in late April, he bounded upstairs to Belle.

"It's bad," he said, his finger poking a section of the newspaper. "Very bad. Guilty. Fourteen years penal servitude to be served in Botany Bay."

Belle screamed.

"My sister, my poor sister! That's what comes of a life of indulgence! My parents are to blame for this, spoiling her while I was sent out to slave away, and running away with that Papist-"

"Where's Tess?" her uncle demanded.

"I don't know. How should I know? She goes for long walks by herself."

Tess was not far away. He espied her out the window, walking by herself across a rocky field toward the house. He went out to meet her.

There, he told her the bad news.

CHAPTER 36

TESS AND ALEX MEET

Alex was also on his way home. He had had an invigorating swim in the cold waters of the tarn. He was walking his horse across the fields when he observed, in the next meadow, Mr. Stowe from the Arms approach a girl in a red bonnet, the poor relative that had come to live with them, as he had heard. He saw him speak with her, and his words must have had some dreadful import, for she crumpled against a tree trunk, her face in her hands, hardly able to support herself. He took a hold of her arm and turning around, indicated his home, but she resisted. Instead, she shook him off and ran away. Mr. Stowe looked after her for a few moments, then shrugged his shoulders in a helpless gesture and returned in the direction of his house.

The girl was running toward Flow Tarn, a dark, deep pool in a steep decline thick with undergrowth. It was known for its current, because of a waterfall that emptied into it. Nobody swam there. He hoped that she was not about to go there in her distress.

His conscience would not allow him to proceed before he knew she was not about to harm herself. He mounted his horse, and diverting by a back lane he knew well, reached the tarn in just a few minutes.

She was there, standing by the side of the water, weeping out loud. Some dreadful distress was upon her. His heart was touched.

"Miss," he said, approaching her side. "Your distress disturbs me. Please tell me you are not about to do yourself any injury here."

She startled to see another person, and Master Alexander at that. He had taken off his hat and was looking at her with large, sincere eyes.

"But I have had very bad news, it is the worst, there is no hope! No hope at all!"

"I am sorry to hear it," he said. "May I be of assistance in any way? Shall I escort you home?"

"No, no." At that, she burst into tears again.

"May I enquire the nature of the news that affects you so deeply, Miss? Has someone died?" Alex was genuinely curious as to what could cause such affliction.

She shook her head.

His rank, his touching concern, and her own need to tell the truth made her say, "My mother has been convicted of a crime she didn't commit, sir, and is being sent away, to the other end of the world - "

The tears overwhelmed her again.

"Transportation! To Van Diemens Land or some such?"

"To Botany Bay. My uncle says she may already be on the way to the prison ship. She didn't do it, sir. We know who did! But that person can't be found! Can you do anything for us, sir?"

It was a desperate plea to any rank or influence he might have above hers. His eyes were filled with pleading.

"If sentence has been passed, there is nothing that can be done," he said gently. "My father has little influence with any judge or court. He is but a farmer. What is her sentence?"

"Fourteen years!" Tears came afresh to her. "It was a set-up, Mr. Bailey."

"I’m very sorry to hear it, Miss - Miss?"

"Woods. Teresa Woods. They call me Tess."

"Tess, your mother hasn't been sentenced to life, and when she returns, she will want to find you safe and well. It would be no solace to her to find out that you had come to harm." Alex had remembered something he had read in a book, a novel where the hero was imprisoned and only the thought of going back to his sweetheart kept him alive through unimaginable terrors. It was a little soppy, but it might appeal to a girl.

"The thought of you may well be what will keep her spirits up during her sentence," he continued strongly. "You must be here to welcome her home. Her life may depend upon it. Do you understand?"

She looked at him curiously.

"Yes, Master Bailey."

"And things might change. She might be able to return early, or something. I shall wait here until I'm sure you are safely away. Go now."

"Yes, Master Bailey," she said, giving him a long, last look before she turned around, and calmer now, made her way up through the thick tangle of ferns until she disappeared from sight.

He went on his way, thinking of her. He had noticed her beautiful dark eyes, slightly almond-shaped, if only they were not brimming with sorrow! Her skin was a shade darker than most English girls, and her red bonnet looked good with her colouring. He found her a little exotic. She reminded him of a tropical flower that might be grown in a rare, carefully-tended garden.

CHAPTER 37

HATING HOLLY

Tess took Alex's words to heart. Though her heart broke at every moment of the day, in her minds, eye she saw her mother thinking about her and looking forward to the day when they could be together again. Perhaps she was now on the ship, consoled only by the thought of Tess.

Her life had taken a nasty turn. Aunt Belle was in a foul mood. She had to earn her keep, she said, because she'd be otherwise a great burden to them in their 'old age'. And since she could sew very well indeed, the boarding houses and hotels thereabouts must have a lot of mending, and she was to go to the inn here and to the surrounding villages and offer herself about.

Tess balked at the idea of going out and asking for employment. She was shy and felt that her appearance was against her. Nevertheless, she made herself tidy and put on her best smile, a false smile because her heart was burdened, and humbly asked for work in several places, including the Reginald Inn at Stagtarn. She received several commissions. Sometimes she worked on the premises, other times, she brought the work home. Her solitary walks helped her a little. Being away from her complaining, fretful aunt was a blessing, though she was often out in heavy rain and made her way through the mists that descended from the hills. On fine days she drank in the lovely views revealed by the sun. It was comforting to see a land so beautifully laid out in gentle hills, deep valleys, streams, and bubbling brooks. No wonder it begat poets and artists.

She thought the owner of The Reginald Inn, Mr. Turnbull, a dour man. He had no charm and took no notice of her. Occasionally, she saw Mrs. Bailey on the premises, asking him to look at a chariot wheel or an axle. She also saw Master Alexander now and then about some business involving his father's carriage, and once he came to get horses for his friends who were visiting. She thought Mr. Turnbull held something against him, because he was distinctly unfriendly, as if wishing him gone. From her vantage point at a large window, she could see a great deal of what was going on in the yard and who was coming and going, and if the window was open, she could hear all too.

Her own heart beat faster when she knew Mr. Alexander was about. He was truly the best young man on earth, and for the first time she knew she was in love.

But to be in love with a man far above her! It was of no use, but it was nice to dream of him as she plied her needle through yards of linen tablecloths and mended holes in the sheets.

Tess knew that her mother would want her to do the very best work that she could do, and she felt that it would please her to know she had exacting standards. Not that she could ever find it out! It was not long before her work became known for its perfection. No irregular seams, no threads left dangling, and the guests who climbed between the patched sheets never even felt the seams.

Mrs. Bailey must have heard of her work though the housekeeper at the Reginald Inn, and the following November, Tess found herself walking up the avenue toward Stagtarn Hall. Her heart was fluttering. Would she see much of Master Alexander? She had never forgotten his good, kind eyes, his concern for her, his willingness to assist her. She day-dreamed about him. But he would never look at her of course. Not in that way. She was ungainly, spotty, and her features, though regular, had nothing striking about them. At least she did not think so.

Mrs. Bailey did not want mending done. She had several new items of napery and had bought the tablecloths and place settings from Manchester and wished them to be edged in lace with a holly sprig motif. Could she do it? Tess nodded.

"These are to be done by Christmas," the housekeeper told her. "There is to be a great party here."

As Tess worked in Stagtarn Hall, she felt reminded of last Christmas, the preparations for the wedding afterwards, the feverish excitement of the family. It was the same here. She did not like the memory and tried to think of other things when the talk among the servants was of decorations, lights, and puddings. The memory of last Christmas was too painful. Had it only been one year ago? It seemed like ten.

I hate Christmas, she said to herself, as she saw the snow fall outside the window onto a little wood of holly trees with bright red berries. *I will never enjoy Christmas again. I will close my eyes, my ears, and my heart to Christmas. It means nothing to me, nothing except sorrow. If I could only escape to a place where Christmas was never heard of!*

Not even a sighting of Mr. Alexander walking though the copse of snow-covered holly could cheer her up!

Deck the halls with boughs of holly. The thread flew through her deft fingers to make the images of the plant she'd come to dislike more than any other as the song refused to leave her head.

CHAPTER 38

CAPTAIN HAMMERSMITH

Stagtarn was full for Christmas. Among the guests was a Captain Frederick Hammersmith, a handsome man about thirty-five, who charmed everybody he met, especially Mrs. Bailey.

She had grown tired of Reginald Turnbull. He had not done what she asked. She was wary of him now. He had formed the idea that she would marry him someday. That was ridiculous! He was insanely jealous of Ephraim and could not understand that, since she had been ready to rid herself of Alexander, she should rid herself of her husband also. He also wanted to acknowledge his daughter Lily by giving her gifts, which she could not sanction.

But Mrs. Bailey had no intention of hurrying Ephraim into the grave. For Ephraim to die while Alexander was still heir? What a mess that would be! Alex would be sure to marry very soon afterwards to ensure his own bloodline.

Ephraim closed his eyes to her lovers, for he was in ill health some of the time, and she was yet a young woman. As long as she did not expose him or his family to public ridicule, he was prepared to accept the situation. He was not even sure that his youngest daughter Lily was his, but he acknowledged her without question.

Mr. Turnbull suspected that he had been thrown over for a handsome captain, and he fumed for months. But later in the year, Captain Hammersmith was posted to Ireland, and in her boredom, Mrs. Bailey took up with Mr. Turnbull again, who meekly took her back.

"Promise you will marry me," he said one summer day when they were lying at the foot of a holm oak in a place known only to themselves. "When the time comes. I'm prepared to wait."

"Oh, we shall see," she said vaguely. "How demanding you are, Reggie! May we not go on as we are?"

"You're not pining for that captain fellow, are you?"

"That man? What put him into your head?" she laughed. "You know you have something to do for me. I have not reneged on that."

Reginald was quiet. He leaned his head back against the tree trunk.

"Did you ask the same commission of the captain?" he asked bitterly. "A professional soldier would be more efficient."

"Now do not be difficult, Reginald, for I hate when a man is difficult."

"I shall not do it, Lydia. You were wrong to even ask it of me, and I was wrong to try."

“I was wrong to ask it of you,” Lydia said. But to herself she said, *“As Old Clary used to say, when you want a job done reet, do it yourself.”*

But she did not dare.

CHAPTER 39

FIVE YEARS LATER

Tess Woods was now acknowledged to be the best seamstress and lacemaker for miles around. She was always busy, and her aunt kept her accounts. She did this because she wanted to know exactly how much Tess could command, and so that she would know if Tess was keeping any for herself. She gave her a little from her earnings for her own use.

Tess wished with all her heart she could move away, back to Preston perhaps, or to try to find her father's family, wherever they were. But this address was where her mother expected her to be. There had been letters, arriving tattered and illegible in parts. Over the course of several, Tess had learned that her mother was serving out her sentence, not in a prison, but by working in a farmhouse in a place called New South Wales. She reported that the weather was hot, the countryside very barren and plain, not at all green and beautiful like England. Her mistress was an ex-convict who had got married and now had four children. She was a good mistress. They were the only two women for miles around and were more like friends than mistress and servant. She was being paid, but there was nothing to buy in this place. The nearest town was ten miles off. The men were very wild. Lots of them never wanted to go back home. She had seen kangaroos and parrots.

Tess thought that she would not tell her if there was any difficulty. The letters were short and written by a stockman called Bert who was not very proficient, but it was a relief to get anything, and she treasured them. Tess wrote back, never saying how depressed and sad she felt all the time. Her Aunt Belle wrote too, and must have said something bad about her, because the next letter contained reproaches about being ungrateful and unhelpful. That hurt her a great deal. In another letter after she turned seventeen, her mother advised her that if she got the chance to marry a man with a good trade, she was to marry. Her mother gave her three bad traits to look out for in a potential husband, if he was mean with money, had a bad temper, and got drunk often, she should not marry him, no matter how charming and handsome he was.

She did not think Alexander Bailey was any of those things, not that she'd ever marry him! She was still secretly in love with him and treasured her chance encounters with him. He had stopped once or twice and asked her how she was.

Alexander's brother Clarence was a different story. He was a wild one, though he was still young. One day, Jeanie's sister, aged fifteen, disappeared. The gossip began, and Uncle Jim had it all to relate upstairs.

It was Master Clarence. He had taken advantage of her, she was with child, and was gone away to have it somewhere. She would never return.

"Then there was that girl in Kirkbride. He ruined her too." Belle remarked, pulling her shawl about her, for it was a chilly evening. She poked the fire.

"I want to ban him from my premises, but if I do, he will find a way to ruin me." Uncle Jim said. "He comes in with his Livingstone cousins, and they have no respect. They have broken furniture, have upended tables full of other mens' drinks, and once set a light to the curtains as a dare."

"So different from young Mr. Bailey," remarked Belle. At the mention of his name, Tess blushed a little. She could not help it. Her aunt saw it and smirked, rolling her eyes upwards. Tess knew this, and setting her sewing down, excused herself, and left the room on the pretext of getting more yarn.

"She thinks she's in love with Mr. Alexander," Belle said to her husband. "No hope there. She isn't even handsome enough to attract a shepherd. How many more years?" She sighed then.

"Her mother could be home with good behaviour," Jim said. He had gotten used to having his niece around and had gotten fond of her.

Belle knew this and it made her resentful.

"Her mother might not come 'ome at all. What are we to do then?"

"You underestimate her, Belle. She's not so bad-looking. When she smiles, she looks 'andsome enough. She'll get a husband."

Tess came back in with her yarn.

"Is there nothing that can be done for poor Amy?" she asked.

"Nothing at all." Belle replied. "She's dead to us all."

"And what of Mr. Clarence? Will he be punished?"

Her uncle shook his head. "No, he will do as he pleases and never face any consequences. It's the way of the world."

CHAPTER 40

BAILEY BALL

The Baileys gave a fine ball in springtime. There was no special reason for it, except that their gentrified neighbours for miles around had given balls, and it was now their turn. It was held on an evening when the moon was full, and from six o'clock onward Mr. Turnbull had watched the fine carriages go past the inn. Some of the guests had come from afar and were staying at Stagtarn Hall. He wondered if Captain Hammersmith was one of them. He had recently returned from Ireland, and he had made himself quite a favourite at the hall again. Lydia had grown cold to him, Reggie, again, and he was seized with an anxious resentment about the handsome captain.

But to his surprise, the captain's carriage stopped, and he asked for a room. Turnbull was pleased, and furnished him the best one he had, and watched him out to the ball a little later on, dressed in splendid dress uniform, and Turnbull's anxiety began all over again.

The captain did not return until the following morning. Mr. Turnbull was livid with jealousy, without having any knowledge if Mrs. Bailey and the captain had even danced. The guest was staying an extra night, and while he was out at Stagharn Hall, of course, Mr. Turnbull searched his room. His dress uniform hung in the wardrobe. As he pulled it to him, the distinct scent, familiar scent, of roses and jasmine wafted to his nostrils, and further searching revealed a crumpled note in his pocket.

'The terrace, in one hour.'

Her scent, her writing. Now a jealous rage consumed him.

CHAPTER 41

HOLLY FIGHT

Two days later, Turnbull rode to the Hall at the time when he knew Mrs. Bailey took her walk in the tall rows of holly trees which screened her from the House.

"Mr. Turnbull, how you frightened me!" was her greeting when he suddenly appeared.

"Mr. Turnbull, Lydia? Am I not Reginald, or Reggie?"

"Mr. Turnbull, please do not begin that again. It distresses me. I am a married woman, and perhaps I regret acting foolishly."

"Foolishly, eh? Why so? Why foolishly?"

"I pray you will keep your voice down! Because we had a connection which was immoral," she said in a forceful whisper

"You were in love with me. You said so. You had my child, Lily Anne. Yet I never see her."

She was silent. Rain clouds had gathered above, and it began to pour heavily upon them.

"I pray you will leave me alone now. I am going inside." She began to walk away, but he followed and grabbed her arm.

"How dare you!" She tried to shake him free.

"How dare you!" he replied, angrily. "You used me."

"Don't be ridiculous, Reggie."

"Is this captain something to you, Lydia? Are you in love with him now?"

"Why do you say such a thing, Mr. Turnbull?"

"You met him on the terrace, did you not? Your perfume is all over his uniform. How did it get there? Did he spill a bottle over himself?"

Now she was very angry. Her face flushed, and she shook herself away with force.

"Let go of me, Reggie."

"You made a fool of me. To think that I risked my neck for you! I know your faithless heart. I can start a rumour, a very wicked rumour."

"You would not dare."

"I would dare. It's well known that you resent Alexander."

"You would not dare," she repeated. But the high colour had fled her face. "You would only implicate yourself." The rain was coming down in sheets now and they were becoming drenched.

"Not necessarily. I can say you requested something of me, and I refused. What do I have to lose? Nothing. You lose all. Your reputation. Your husband, for while he may put up with your dalliances, will he put up with rumours that you tried to have Alexander murdered? He could well punish you by casting you and Clarence out into the cold."

"Master Clarence to you. Now get away from me," she hissed. "Go!"

He left her. He was conscious of having wounded her, making her frightened. He felt satisfied in a way, but there was no peace.

He knew that they would never speak again, and he would forever be kept from his only child, and the prospect shattered his heart.

CHAPTER 42

MOTHER AND CLARENCE

"Good morning, Mother." Clarence pecked his mother's cheek. "Is luncheon going to be soon? I have to go out again."

"Why is that, son? You're never in now. I told you, time and again, that one day you may inherit this, and your father has to see you interested. You should spend the afternoon with him in the fields."

"Mother, give up. There is no hope. I rather wish you had never told me that I would get all this, and it would be Livingstone property again. It will never happen. All through my childhood, you kept saying it, and impressing upon me to keep it secret. I thought some quirk of the law would make it happen, but now I know it's hopeless. I do wish you hadn't misled me, Mother. This place will never belong to me."

"You must not say that." Her voice was sharp.

"But how, Mama? How? Alex is in the way. How to push him out?"

"I don't know."

"It's so maddening." Clarence paced about the room. "I want it so badly, and he doesn't care one way or another. He has no ambition. He's happy with a library full of books and a swim every day, rain or shine. Now Father wishes me to go into the Army. He's talking about buying me a commission."

"What? He never mentioned it to me!"

"Did he not? Rumours have reached him about some larking about, and I suppose he thinks some military training would do me good."

"Clarence," she said slowly. "I have had a thought of late. If you really want this house and land enough, you must be prepared to take it for yourself."

"How, Mother? What is your thought?"

He listened to her speak at length, and his eyes were rapt with attention.

"Would it not be very wrong, Mother? I mean -"

"It is the only way. Can you think of another? Just think of all the kings and queens of history who had to make life and death decisions to take what was theirs, and often, what was not, not just for themselves, but for their countrymen. Did they wonder if it was wrong?"

"My half-brother," he muttered.

"Do not think of him as your brother. He is your enemy. It's Livingstone land."

"It shall be done, Mother! We'll get our land back! Our land! I shall not do it just for myself, but for future generations of Livingstones! I can do no less for my children and my grandchildren."

"I knew you would see it the correct way, dear. Your grandfather would be very proud of you."

CHAPTER 43

DISGUISED

She chose a Saturday evening. There would be people about shopping for Sunday, and many witnesses. She would spend the week working the staff hard cleaning the house top to bottom, and then she'd give them that afternoon off as a reward. Ephraim would be away on business for the day. He had to see his banker in Carlisle. She arranged for her daughters to be away for the week at the Livingstone cousins, out of the way of brooms, carpet beaters, and dust. They would not return until Sunday, and the governess would take a holiday.

But what of the grooms and stable hands? She would be generous and give them that afternoon off also.

The butler and housekeeper? Would they be suspicious? Would Mrs. Freely just stay in her apartments? If she did, it would be all right. And Mr. Grogan? She would give him some money to take himself to Penrith where his old mother lived.

She came in to lunch, a cold buffet set out by Maggie and the housemaids before they had left.

"Where's Clarence?" Alex asked when he came in.

"He went with your father," she said. "At the last minute, he elected to go."

Alex thought it strange. Clary never offered himself to their father's business. He helped himself to soup and cold ham.

There was only the two of them. They did not converse easily together, and never had. But Mrs. Bailey was ready. "Alex," said she, "I have a problem with my account book. I have gotten myself so mixed up, adding and subtracting, and the correct sum is not coming out at all. Could I trouble you to look at it this afternoon? For at the end of the month, as you know, it needs to be all in order. I am so muddled."

Alex hesitated. He was going to go for a ride over to Little Orton to see a friend there. But that could wait.

"Yes, Mother."

Good. He will be out of the way, in my dressing room. Examining the books to find errors I deliberately put in there.

An hour later Alexander seated himself at the small table in his stepmother's dressing room, adjacent to her bedchamber. Dressing-room was a misnomer. Though it had a sofa, it was a private study where she wrote and answered letters, and of course, did her household accounts. He took down the ledger, and armed with several sheets of paper and pencils, began to pore over columns headed with the words Household, Groceries, Wages, Dress Allowances, and others.

Clarence, who had kept to his room all this time, bored and cross, was already on his way to Alexander's chamber. His mother joined him there.

"I'm hungry, Mother," he complained.

"Never mind that. This is important. His dark blue coat, this hat, that paisley muffler." It was chilly, and the muffler would half-conceal his face.

"What of the horse, Mother?"

"I sent the boys off too. You go and get her yourself. You'll have to saddle her up."

"Oh, I shall manage all that. But I don't like his mare. He treats her too gently, and she doesn't know discipline." Dressed now in Alexander's coat and boots, she pulled the muffler up about his ears and his hat down.

"Do not choose today to teach Gaia. You must ride as he does, the same pace. Remember, you are he. Ride high in the saddle, no slouching, no leaning forward, and if a tradesman or a cottager salutes you, salute him back. You do not have to speak it, a nod will do. Alexander always acknowledges a greeting."

"Yes, Mother. Alex is such a favourite around here, it seems a shame to hang him."

"Do you want this land or do you not?" she demanded.

"Oh, of course I do. I'm just nervous. Are you sure it will be all right? Wish me luck, Mother."

"When you get to the yard, toss the boy a sixpence and tie up Gaia yourself at the railing near the door as he forages on the ground for it. And one last thing, son. Make sure it is done before you hasten away. If you have to wait a few moments, it will be worth it for your and my peace of mind, and then hasten home by the back lanes."

"Yes, Mother."

She kissed him and he was gone.

The dappled grey mare did not like him. She knew it was not Alexander. But after an initial rocky beginning, he managed to calm her and set off for the village, there to be seen by everybody as Master Alexander Bailey on his horse, and several people saw horse and rider turn in to the Reginald Arms.

CHAPTER 44

TESS SEES MURDER

The rain was beginning, and Tess wondered if she should wait until Monday to deliver her mending. But she liked to get rid of her work as soon as it was done. So, she donned her bonnet and cloak and set off, her basket of linen clasped to her side.

The first place she reached was Reginald's Inn. The housekeeper was usually busy on Saturdays, and Tess knew she could leave the linen in the cupboard which was located around the corner a little way from the office where Mr. Reginald sat. If there was no guest about, she used the front door.

"Who is there?" he asked as she passed in.

"Tess Woods, Mr. Turnbull. I'm leaving some linen for Mrs. Mahony."

"All right," was the reply. "Shut the door after you when you go. It's cold."

"Yes, sir." She passed by and put her linen in the cupboard, in the correct places, sheets here, tablecloths there, Mr. Turnbull's shirt on a hanger, and a few table napkins near the tablecloths.

She heard somebody come hurriedly in the front door. A pause. Then a deafening noise exploded nearby. A gunshot! Then a loud groan, then a second shot. Then nothing. For a moment she was paralyzed in fright, her hands covering her ears. Had it really been a gunshot?

She ran to see what was afoot. Mr. Turnbull's door was open. An appalling sight met her. Mr. Turnbull was on the floor, his eyes open and staring, his chest oozing blood. She recoiled, horrified. Kneeling over him, with his back to her, was a gentleman in a dark blue coat and top hat. He had his finger on Mr. Turnbull's neck as a doctor would, and by his side was a pistol. It looked like, – but it could not be, – Alexander Bailey!

She screamed. The startled man looked up and around at her. The muffler fell. It was not Alexander, but his brother Clarence! He looked at her with grim shock, then got up in a menacing way, taking his pistol, and she fled.

"Murder, murder!" she cried as she ran out the front door, terrified now that she would be next. She saw Alexander's mare tied to the railing. She had been unsettled by the noise and was neighing. Tess ran around the corner of the building. Shouts followed, the alarm had been raised. Then the horse whinnied in sudden pain or fright, and hooves galloped away.

Mr. Turnbull was dead, and one of the sheets only just put into the cupboard was taken from there and spread over his body.

There was no constable in the village, nor a doctor. Mrs. Mahony took charge of Tess and forced some brandy through her lips, and then sent for her uncle to take her home. She walked with him in a daze. Had she really seen what she had seen? Master Clarence Bailey had murdered Mr. Turnbull in cold blood. No words had been exchanged that she had heard, no quarrel.

Clarence reached home safely by the back roads, let himself in the servants' entrance, and slipped up to his own room. Her mother was there. She had his own clothes waiting for him.

"Is it done?"

"It is done. Very straightforward."

"Are you sure he is -?"

"Very sure."

"Did anybody see you?"

"Yes, the girl from the arms. She came in. She saw me. But she wouldn't know me from Alexander, and while I went through the village on my way there, at least two people called out to me as 'Master Alexander."

"The muffler would have hidden you."

He did not want to tell her that it had slipped, revealing him.

"What do we do now, Mother?"

"We must wait. You and I know nothing of any of this until we are told. Come. Get changed quickly and we will go downstairs. Your father will be home very soon"..."

CHAPTER 45

DEVILS FROM HELL

As Ephraim Bailey rode through the village that evening, he was hailed by a few tradesmen who enjoined him to halt and told him what had happened, and that young Mr. Bailey had been seen in the village and went into the Reginald yard. Shots had been fired, and he was seen leaving again by the back, at a gallop.

"My son Alexander!" he said in utter astonishment

"But sir," said Arkins, the cobbler. "Miss Tess Woods, as lives at the arms with the Stowes, she was at the scene and saw Mr. Clarence, not Mr. Alexander. She was very sure of it."

He felt sick. He went into the Reginald and inspected the body of the deceased, now laid out on his own bed upstairs. The deceased man's brothers were expected any moment from Bowness, so he did not delay.

The doctor had visited and pronounced two wounds to the chest had killed Mr. Turnbull and had departed saying that he would have to inform the coroner.

He rode home as fast as he could, and before he took off his greatcoat and hat, he roused his fittest coachman and told him to take the carriage with four horses to his attorney at Carlisle. He wrote him a note telling him that he was needed at Stagtarn that very night. Ephraim knew that the magistrate would be upon them on Monday, if not Sunday, and he wanted to be prepared with legal advice. He strode upstairs to dress for dinner - no matter how serious the crisis, the proprieties had to be kept. His man had been in the village and told him anew about the shooting but offered no information as to who could have done it.

The servants had already brought the news of the death to Stagtarn, but they had been afraid to say who the murderer was rumoured to be. They took it personally that it was one of their gentlemen who was suspected of a foul deed. After all, though he had been seen coming through the village, none of them had seen Mr. Alexander do it! A few of them had seen him ride through the village and then the boy Jones from the Reginald had reported that Mr. Alexander had gone in to see Mr. Turnbull. He had heard a shot, and then Mr. Alex had run out, mounted his horse, whipped her to a gallop and left via the back gates. He had had to jump out of the mare's way, but this they kept to themselves.

As Alexander went into the drawing room, Clarence and his stepmother were there before him.

"You went to Carlisle?" he asked Clarence.

"No, I turned back after a short distance. It would have been a crashing bore with Father."

"It was not boring here. There was shocking news. Have you not heard? Mr. Turnbull of the Reginald Inn was murdered."

"That's dreadful. Who shot him?"

"If I were a detective, I would pounce upon your words, Clary, for I never said he was shot."

"Is not that the usual way to murder somebody?" Clarence said.

Their mother was saying nothing at all, but she seemed to be anxious. The bad news had unnerved her, she said. Murder in a small village! She sat, clasping and unclasping her hands, her face drawn in worry.

Ephraim entered the drawing room.

"I have had the most dreadful news coming through the village," he said, panting heavily, turning from one son to another.

"About Mr. Turnbull. We know it." Alexander said. "It was a cruel murder."

"And of you, Alexander."

"Of me? Of what are you speaking, Father?"

"Yes, you. You were reported to have gone into the Reginald, shots were heard, and then you emerged and galloped away, nearly running over the stableboy. You, Alexander! What was that? I want the truth! Were you there this afternoon?"

"That's preposterous! I spent two hours going over Mother's accounts."

His father swung around to his second son.

"But then, I heard too, that someone recognised you, Clarence," he said, pointing a finger at him.

"Father, that's a lie. I was not there."

"After you left Father, where did you go? I did not see you here," Alexander said.

"What do you mean, after you left me? You were not with me this afternoon!"

"There, you lied." Alexander said, rising from his chair. "What is going on? Why was I supposed to have been in the village when I was not there?"

"I lied. I was not here, I was with a friend. A person of the fairer sex." Clarence said bluntly. He turned to his mother. "Sorry, Mother, I lied to you about going with Father."

"Please, let us all be calm," Mrs. Bailey said. "There is some dreadful mistake." She said no more. The news that Clarence had been recognised hit her like a tree falling upon her head. Her mouth felt dry, her heart hammered in her breast. *Who saw him?*

A cold dinner awaited them on the sideboard, which did not please Ephraim either as they served themselves and took their places.

"Why was it necessary to give Cook the afternoon off?" he demanded. He had become less good humoured as the years had gone by. His was not a happy marriage. There was deceit and selfishness. Lydia found he was not at all as malleable as he had been when they had been newly married, and she often nagged him. Constant pains in his head and neck made him short-tempered also.

"Cook worked so hard during the week, scrubbing the kitchen."

"I do not believe you. There's something very odd going on here. A murder was committed, and both of our sons were reported to be on the scene," he said to her hotly.

"And as for you, you are unnaturally calm. I find your attitude very strange. Thankfully, I have already sent for Moore. He should be here before ten o'clock. Nobody is to retire until we have decided the truth of this and made some sort of plan. This could be the end of us all."

"I was not there," Alexander was angry. "Mother, was I not in your dressing room for hours?"

"I left you to yourself there, Alex. You could have left the house, for all I know." Her voice was very low.

Alex looked at her speechlessly. She was not looking at him. He was strongly reminded of that time he had returned after he had almost drowned at Thora Tarn. It hit him like a jolt, a blow to his chest. She had not looked at him then, either. She had been very ill-at-ease.

He suddenly understood everything.

"You've plotted this," he said in a raised voice. "You have plotted this. That was Clarence, disguised as me, and on my horse, I wager. You wanted people to believe that I did it? Why?"

Ephraim was speechless, but his wife's and son's silence said more than any words.

After some time, he spoke. His tone was like a sharp knife, his words chosen carefully.

"I do not want to see this family's name dragged through the courts, through the mud of every newspaper in the kingdom. You, Madam, you have three daughters who will end up as nobodies in society, shunned and scorned by all. If you do not care about them, I do. This is about Livingstone land, is it not?"

Alex paled. He saw his stepmother for the first time as she really was.

"I have wanted this since we married," she retorted, her voice now full of venom. "Yes, I wanted this land for my own son, who has Livingstone blood! When I married you, he was not supposed to live." She pointed at a shocked Alexander. "But he did."

"You arranged that I drown at Thora Tarn!" Alex shouted.

"I did not!" But Alexander did not believe her.

“You were in a state of shock when I came back.”

“I was worried about you, and relief hit me.”

“Lies!” Alexander said, and Clarence rose.

“Do not speak to my mother like that!”

His father rose also from the table, picked up a carafe of wine, and with all his strength smashed it against the far wall. The sound of shattering glass jolted everybody. A large stain of claret red dripped down the white wallpaper. The door burst open. A footman stood there, and Ephraim shouted, "Leave us!"

Nobody spoke after that. Clarence sat again. The room darkened, no candle was lit, and it seemed to Alex and his father that every evil spirit from Hell was present and weighed down upon them, so heavy, oppressive, and ugly was the very air they breathed.

Alex got up quietly and left the room. He could not bear to even look at his stepmother and Clary. He felt a searing sense of betrayal in his breast. Clary! His own brother! Clary plotted against him! Hated him as much as Cain hated Abel!

He staggered rather than walked up the stairs, shut himself in his room, and alone, gave way to sobs.

CHAPTER 46

MARRIAGE ARRANGED

Tess had received such a great shock that after she returned home, she had to go to bed. Annie brought her tea and a hot water jar, and after that she tried to sleep, but the scene played over and over in her mind.

It was Clarence, of that she was sure. Clarence in a blue greatcoat and paisley muffler, dressed as his brother. Clarence, as Alexander, killed Mr. Turnbull.

"Why? Why?" There was no reply. She eventually fell into a disturbed sleep.

It was eleven o'clock when Mr. Stowe had a surprise visit from Mr. Bailey in the Stagtarn Arms. He was accompanied by a respectably dressed little man with round spectacles. Mr. Stowe was gathering up glasses at the time.

"I need to see you as a matter of urgency," said Mr. Bailey quietly.

Guessing that it had something to do with the afternoon's tragic events, Mr. Stowe set down his glasses and invited them into the snuggery.

"We would prefer to speak in the privacy of your own apartments, and this is something your wife may wish to hear also," said Mr. Bailey.

Mystified, he opened the connecting door and led them upstairs. Belle was surprised to see the gentlemen, and she quickly brought two more chairs to the fire. Mr. Stowe poured the gentlemen a whiskey each.

"Your niece was at the scene of the unfortunate murder today," began Mr. Ephraim. "It appears that one of my sons was involved in that heinous occurrence, and that she saw him clearly, or so she has said."

He paused, and the Stowes nodded.

"Your niece is an important witness. Did she recognise who was at the victim's side?"

"She did."

"Very well." Mr. Bailey took a very deep breath. "I wish to preserve my family at all costs, Mr. Stowe, and therefore I wish to make you an offer. But perhaps I should allow my respected friend to explain why."

"Under English Common Law," said Mr. Moore, rattling off several codes that went over their heads, "a wife may not testify against her husband."

Mr. and Mrs. Stowe looked quickly at each other.

"Are you proposing for our niece?" asked Mrs. Stowe.

"Yes, I am."

"For which?"

"For whichever of my sons she saw by the dead man's side."

"She said it was - but I shall ask her," cried Mrs. Stowe. "I shall ask her, now. She is resting, after the great shock."

There was silence among the men as she pattered quickly up the stairs.

Tess was awake. She had heard voices downstairs. She sat up in bed when her aunt came in. Quickly setting the candle down, her voice quivering with excitement, Belle told her what was afoot.

"I don't understand. What does this mean? What are you talking about?" Tess asked.

Belle was so short of breath she could hardly explain, but she managed to get it out in some coherent fashion, and it dawned upon Tess that she had been asked for in marriage. And to one of the brothers, whichever one had done the foul deed, because it would protect him from prosecution and the hangman's noose.

"What a great thing for you, Tess, for all of us, and for your mother when she returns! To see you settled far above your station! Oh, so far above!"

"No, no, Aunt. This is too sudden. I can't -"

"Nonsense! You have a little fancy for young Mr. Bailey, Mr. Alexander, I know you have. Say it was him, and he will be yours! He is a gentle, kind soul! Oh, you will have a generous dress allowance, and all that he is to inherit! Say it was Mr. Alexander!"

Tess was suddenly very tempted. Could she - could she marry the man of her dreams simply by saying that she had seen him commit murder? But no!

"I cannot say it was Alexander, Aunt Belle. It was not Alexander, it was his brother Clarence."

"Oh, you little fool! Why can you not do the best thing for yourself?"

"Because he did not do it. He is no murderer! How would he ever have any love or respect for me, if I pointed my finger at him and called him a murderer? If I love him, I must tell the truth. It was Mr. Clarence, but I shall not marry Mr. Clarence. You may go down and tell them." She slid down underneath the covers and covered her head.

"You ungrateful wretch! I will not tell them any such thing! You will marry Mr. Clarence, and you shall not leave this room until you agree!"

"When I am asked by the constable who I saw, I shall say 'Mr. Clarence Bailey,'" she said in a muffled voice. "And he will hang for the crime. If you could have only beheld the terrible thing that met my eyes, Aunt Belle! I can't sleep for thinking of poor Mr. Turnbull!"

There was silence for a moment.

"Tess, I have the solution." Her aunt shook her shoulder. "You shall say tonight it was Alexander and marry him tomorrow. Then you will have him, but on Monday, you will tell the magistrate that it was Mr. Clarence! What a clever thing to do!"

"No, Aunt. How could Mr. Alexander ever respect me for lying like that? It would be a dreadful deceit, and then there would always be the question that Alexander persuaded me perhaps to name his brother, and people would always think he lied too! No, I shall not do it!"

"You obstinate, ungrateful wench! I shall write your mother this instant! Think how aggrieved she will feel! How are you to support her when she returns? From this moment on, unless you agree to marry Mr. Clarence, though I would much prefer Mr. Alexander, you will be turned out of this house and onto the street! There you may beg for your bread or become a prostitute, for all I care!" She stamped away, calmed herself as she went downstairs, and entered the living room with a smile on her face.

"She said it was Mr. Clarence, and she is willing to marry him."

Ephraim rose hastily from his chair.

"Good! I will see that she, and you, are taken care of handsomely. Now this wedding must happen before Monday, for the magistrate will be here then. She will be legally entitled to remain silent. He will not be able to ask her a thing. She will tell him, 'It was not Alexander, sir.' And that will suffice. He may ask no more! Oh, thank you, Mr. Stowe. Thank you, Mrs. Stowe. Such a service you have rendered me tonight! I have a pastor in mind who will do the job. He is a poor curate, and I will send for him tomorrow morning. We shall have an afternoon ceremony, at Stagtarn Hall. Three o'clock. Moore will prepare all the legalities."

With that, the gentlemen left. Mr. and Mrs. Stowe were speechless at first, before bursting into gales of laughter.

"We're made up, made up for life!" Jim rubbed his hands. "He's giving me five hundred pounds!"

"Five hundred! But you can't say a thing about it, it sounds as if we sold her. Oh, five hundred pounds!"

"Think what we can do, Belle! Retire next year, maybe!"

"Yes, but why won't she say 'Alexander?' She'd be rich as Croesus!"

"Be thankful she will marry one of them, Belle."

"Oh dear!"

"What is it?"

"She did not agree or give her consent. I told a fib to the gentlemen, but of course, she will. She will. If I have to drug her with opium, dress her myself, drag her to that altar, hide behind her, and pop up and say 'I do' at the proper time, I'll see she marries Mr. Clarence Bailey tomorrow afternoon at three o'clock!"

They downed a whiskey each, and then another, and then humming a lively country song, they danced about the living room.

Tess heard the levity and guessed the truth. Her heart plummeted to her toes.

CHAPTER 47

ALEX AND DAD CHAT

"I must marry? Father, I am only eighteen! I'm not going to marry!" Clarence was very angry.

"You have to. Mr. Moore?" The little man again explained why, again listing the legal codes.

"Marry that sewing wench?" Clarence was horrified.

"That girl who saw you, yes, the seamstress."

"Her? Marry her? I will not marry her. Who is she? Nobody! And she is older than me!"

"You will marry her, or she will give evidence against you."

"Why did you not just pay for her silence?" asked his mother, furious also.

"Because that is not enough to ensure her silence," said Ephraim.

"Why did you not threaten her? You are a stupid man," Lydia said to him. Her entire body trembled with anger.

Ephraim considered this. He did not believe that she had anything much to do with it. Alex was wrong. To contemplate that his wife was evil, that she had planned a murder, nay, two, was far too much for his weary mind. But she had shown no concern that Alexander's life had been in danger from his own brother. None at all.

She guessed his thoughts.

"Oh, I see," she said with contempt. "It pleases you to see my son married to a plain, ugly girl who has no breeding, no name, uneducated, and doesn't know a knife from a fork."

"She is ugly," Clarence said. He had a fleeting memory of the face looking so shocked at his own, a darkish, spotty complexion, big frightened eyes, mouth open like an imbecile.

"She is pockmarked," his mother said cattily.

"Do not expect any grandchildren, for I shall not go near her," Clarence said. He was fuming. He should have been happy tonight. How had it all gone so wrong?

"You do not know how lucky you are," his father snapped. "You deserve hanging. I will remember this day for the rest of my life. I am going to bed."

He clumped up the stairs, candle in hand. He paused as he passed Alexander's room, knocked, and hearing an answer, went in.

"Are you all right, son?"

"Yes, sir."

Mr. Bailey sat down heavily on the chair beside the bed.

"I'm sorry for all this," he said.

"It's not your fault, Father."

There was silence, broken only by a heavy sigh from Mr. Bailey.

"Father?"

"Yes?"

"What was my mother like? You have never spoken to me of my mother."

Ephraim remembered the slim smiling girl with the fair hair and gentle nature. He had known her since childhood, and fresh in his bereavement from his first wife, knew that her love and tenderness could heal him. Alexandra Grant had loved him all of her life. He began to speak of her. When he began, he could not stop.

Memories flooded him. An hour passed. He finally finished.

"Thank you, Father."

"You're a good son, Alex. Will you be present tomorrow?"

"If I have to be."

"I will leave it up to you."

They said goodnight, and he went to bed. Tomorrow would be a full day. Alex lay in bed, thinking. The betrayal of his brother and stepmother was uppermost in his mind. Then he thought about the girl he had met by the dangerous waterfall, that day some years ago. Her distress. Her hard life. Her mother being a convict. He had never told anybody. He would never tell anybody. How had she consented to this farce of a marriage? He had thought her a girl of some depth and feeling, and he was disappointed.

She'd smiled shyly at him a few times since when their paths had crossed, and it had occurred to him more than once that she had a little fancy for him. He still thought of an exotic flower when he beheld her, for she favoured strong, vibrant colours, and they suited her.

She was to become his brother's wife tomorrow.

CHAPTER 48

WEDDING

Belle was not joking about the opium. Tess got up and ate porridge laced with it and never noticed. She was soon limp, falling asleep as she sat over her tea.

"What 'ave you done, Ma'am?" Annie asked in surprise.

"What I had to do, and no more lip from you. Help me get her upstairs and dressed. Her best gown, the one she made herself."

"What is this about, Ma'am?"

"She's going somewhere important. I told you, no more lip, no more questions. It's for her own good."

Tess felt that she was in a dream. There was a thick cloud over her mind, and her body was tired. Her limbs were heavy. She was conscious of her aunt and Annie dressing her in her Sunday gown, a full-skirted cerise and grey plaid poplin she had made herself, with a white bodice and collar to match the skirt. They put the grey bonnet with the cerise ribbon upon her head, gloves on her hands, her best boots on her feet, and rubbed some colour onto her face. Then she was put into a hackney carriage and brought out of the village, up the Long Road to Stagtarn Hall. She was taken in the front door and led into the drawing room on the left. There was a clergyman in his vestments there with a book. And Mr. Bailey, and Mrs. Bailey. The tables had several empty glasses, and bottles of spirits lay about.

She saw Clarence, the murderer, standing by the priest.

Then she remembered. They had brought her here to marry Clarence!

"No!" she sobbed. The curate looked away. The sum he had been offered for this service equalled his stipend for the entire year. It would enable him to marry his sweetheart.

Her uncle took her arm firmly in his and brought her to Clarence's side. He looked upon her with contempt.

The curate began to read from his book. She did not hear his words.

She was getting married today.

She heard a movement behind her. She looked around, and she saw Alexander. He was only a few feet from her. His eyes were kind and blue, and he gave her a small, sad smile. Her eyes filled with tears before she lowered them and turned her head to the celebrant.

Seven minutes later, after somehow making the responses expected of her, but not without several pinches in the arm from her aunt, she was Mrs. Clarence Bailey.

A little while before that, Alexander had, from an upper window, watched Mr. and Mrs. Stowe lead the bride from the closed carriage toward the front steps of the house. They seemed to have to hold her up and steady her. She seemed drugged. Of course she was. What woman would freely consent to marry a murderer, even if he was wealthy? She was at the mercy of the greedy couple. He resolved to go to the ceremony out of pity for her, and because she might need a friend there, someone who cared about her.

Stop, Alexander, he said to himself, when he realised that he thought of her with something like affection. *'Thy brother's wife'*. No, he would only be her friend. She was to be part of his family, and if he could, he would help her settle in to what was going to be a very difficult situation. He hoped though, that his father would send him away to live elsewhere. The situation between him and his brother was an impossible one. Alex was not afraid of his stepmother. He knew that if anything happened to him now, his father would have no mercy upon her. He had told him so. He had briefly considered making himself absent, but why should he? This was his home. Neither was he afraid of his brother Clarence, who would hardly risk the hangman again.

I ought to marry, he thought to himself. I *ought to marry and have children. Then it would all go away from the Livingstones.*

But he had never met a young lady he liked enough to marry.

CHAPTER 49

POST WEDDING

Drinks were poured and taken by all. Her drink made Tess feel very ill, and after a few sips, she set down her glass. Then her uncle and aunt stood up to take their leave.

She practically ran after them, staggering to catch up with them on the front steps. She swayed and held the doorpost for support.

"Don't leave me here!" she whispered.

"Be a dutiful wife, Tess, and submit to your husband." Belle said. Then she giggled suddenly, and they departed. Tess wandered back into the house. Nobody was taking any notice of her at all. Her husband of an hour was not to be found, and her parents-in-law had disappeared somewhere also.

Alexander was in the drawing room, standing by the fireplace, smoking. He nodded politely to her, looked down at his feet, and then said, "I am sorry you are in this situation. Your feelings about this marriage are very clear to me. You have no friend in my half-brother or in my parents, and I feel it necessary to advise you. My half-brother has said he will not consummate the marriage, and if I were you, I would keep him to it," he said awkwardly, his head still down. "That way, if you want to get an annulment, you would have some grounds." He threw his cigar into the fire and left the room quickly.

An annulment! She may not be tied for life after all! Hope surged.

The girls were brought down by their bewildered governess and introduced to their sister-in-law. It was an indication of how tawdry this whole affair was that they had not been dressed up and at the ceremony downstairs. Though they curtsied, they looked warily at her and even critically. Tess saw three girls in pretty frocks and ribbons, well-behaved but not friendly. For all their youth, they knew that she was not of their rank, and not a gentleman's daughter. The youngest looked at her saucer-eyed, the middle girl giggled, and the older one wrinkled her nose. Clary's wife was nobody!

She still did not know where she was to sleep, but her little bundle of belongings was gone, and it must be somewhere. She asked one of the maids, who brought her to a small room at the end of a long corridor. A fire burned in the grate. She was very glad to shut the door, and silently thanked whoever it was who had provided her with a little sanctuary. She took out her treasures, her father's missal, a few books, her mother's letters and her clothes and the few ornaments she possessed.

The room had been Mrs. Bailey's doing, and her intention was to keep her as far away from Clary as possible. The thought of polluting the Livingstone line with low progeny was anathema to her. This marriage would be in name only until it was time to beget an heir. Fortunately, Clarence was repelled by her!

Tess did not appear to dinner. She did not know what the bell she heard was for, and a tray was taken up with a good dinner upon it, and some coffee. She went to bed early and was undisturbed.

CHAPTER 50

THE HOLLY MAZE

She rose on Monday and dressed in an everyday gown, forest green wool with a cream sprig, and affixed a long collar of cream lace and went downstairs. She was shown to the breakfast room and helped herself from the sideboard. Only her parents-in-law were there. The food was good and plentiful. She watched what Mrs. Bailey did and followed suit. Her father-in-law nodded to her and said he hoped she had slept well, and she said she had. She ate in silence, looking out the large window with raindrops streaming down outside.

Mrs. Bailey was immersed in her own thoughts. There was one hope left for her to secure the estate for the

Livingstone line. After breakfast, there was a break in the rain, and she asked Tess to take a turn with her in the holly walk. It was like a maze. The holly leaves shone with raindrops.

"Are you sure it was my son Clarence you saw?" she asked her.

"Mrs. Bailey, is not that the reason I married him yesterday?"

"Everybody in the village saw young Mr. Bailey, that is, Mr. Alexander Bailey. Everybody. It would not be too odd, you know, if you saw him too."

Tess reacted with horror. She saw what Mrs. Bailey's motive was in speaking to her thus.

It was the reverse of what her Aunt Belle had suggested.

"I shall tell the magistrate it was not Master Alexander if he asks me," she said calmly.

"You could have a very comfortable and happy life here, if you chose differently," said her mother-in-law with an edge to her voice. "I think you only *thought* you saw Clarence, because you did not *want* to see Alexander. Is not that it? I can read you, Teresa. I saw your look to Mr. Alexander yesterday in the drawing room. You do not wish to say it was him, because you think you are in love with him. He does not love you. He never will. Come now, I am a generous woman. You will never want for anything as Clarence's wife and mistress of this house, which you will be in time if you do as I suggest. You made a mistake." She took her arm in a warm gesture.

"I made no mistake, Ma'am. I saw Mr. Clarence," Tess said quietly, though feeling humiliated that she was so transparent in her affections. The woman's arm felt like a rope around hers, and she had a strong urge to shake it off.

"Very well then! I shall leave you here to find your own way out." Mrs. Bailey dropped her arm and walked quickly away, and Tess walked on.

"Thank you." A few moments later, the voice made her spin around. She had very confused feelings to see Alexander there, and by his side, was Annie Ware in her hat and shawl, carrying her box and beaming.

"I could not but hear that exchange." Alexander said. "I knew she would speak to you. I went out early and fetched Annie from your uncle's house, so that I should have a witness. This maze is where she conducts her business." He was blushing a little as he spoke, and there was a light in his eye.

"I've left the Arms! I'm to be your maid," Annie said gleefully. "I could not stand what your uncle and aunt done to you, marrying a man you don't like, and who is as likely to murder you as he murdered Mr. Turnbull. I'm to sleep in your room." Evidently everything had been explained to Annie, and she had taken on the task of being her guard.

"We hope it shall not come to murder," Alexander said hurriedly. "But yes, Annie is to be your maid. You need one. I spoke with my father this morning. You are to have a better room. You are to have a clothes allowance, and I suppose you will be busy ordering materials from London and going to mantua makers."

"She does not need mantua makers," Annie said scornfully. "Miss Tess, er, Mrs. Bailey, is better than anybody with 'er needle, she is. She could make the Queen's wardrobe."

"I will show you the way out of this maze," Alexander said then. There was something about the way this intention reached Tess' ears that caused her heart to soar with hope. Did it have another meaning? She glanced at him. He met her glance with a gentle look of his own and offered her his arm, which she gladly took.

He evidently did not mind too much overhearing that she was in love with him, Tess thought. Annulment, come at the soonest!

The magistrate visited later on with two constables, and she answered truthfully about what she saw, just falling short of saying it was her husband Clarence, as was expected of her. It was most definitely not Mr. Alexander, she said. He did not look in the least like Mr. Alexander. She was absolutely certain of that. Mr. Blundell was satisfied. He did not relish the prospect of arresting a gentleman, and after downing several ports, while the constables had none, he departed.

. . .

Mrs. Bailey gave her a look of extreme contempt and hatred, and with a deliberate swish of her crinoline, left the room.

"She hates us both, now," Alexander said to her sotto-voce.

"Can she harm us?"

"I do not know." Alexander looked a little wary. "If harm came to either of us, I think it would look bad for her."

CHAPTER 51

CLARY DEPRESSED

Annie slept in her mistress's room. Clarence did not try to gain entry, but he was worried. The possibility of an annulment had occurred to him as long as the marriage had not been consummated. Would he be safe as a free man?

He was a very discontented. His thoughts were full of bitterness. All his life there had been one influence upon him, that of his mother. She had promised him something he could never have. He had committed murder for it, and the crime haunted him day and night. He asked himself how he would have felt if Alexander were to hang. Would he have had a happy life with all the land and the house, knowing the price that had been exacted for it?

"I do not know what to do now," his mother admitted as they walked in the holly trees. "I have tried everything!"

"We should let it go then, Mother. God is against us. But what shall I do? I have no profession, and I shall have to go to Oxford or Edinburgh to study. I will not be Alexander's land agent, as many younger brothers do. I shall go away, I think."

"If you do, you have to take your wife with you. I do not want her here. Her aunt and uncle visit, and they make me ill. Uncouth, and rolling in money now because your father bribed them to hand her over."

"I do not know where to go. I bet the other fellows at Oxford haven't wives dragging them down."

The Reginald Inn was sold to a hotelier who refurbished it top to bottom to attract the cream of society to Cumberland, for with more and more towns and cities being linked by railway lines, more tourists were coming to see the Lakes. It became a very comfortable hotel.

Tess was not as unhappy in her new life as would be expected. She feared her mother-in-law, and was in awe of her father-in-law, but was at ease when Alexander was there. Clarence never spoke to her except when necessary, and she never spoke to him. In her heart, she did not feel married, and Alexander went out of his way to have a few friendly words with her whenever he could.

She was very surprised, and pleased, to see that her complexion had greatly improved since she had come to Stagtarn. There was fresh fruit on the table at every meal, and she loved peaches and apricots. She did not know how they were obtained, but evidently rich people could have anything they wanted at any time of the year. Her spots disappeared. Jane, the housemaid, told her that her skin was clear and bright. Tess had heard Mrs. Baddelley describe people with good skin as having a 'luminous complexion,' so she wondered if she now had that.

"Do you have any news of your mother?" Alexander asked her one day.

He remembers! Tess was secretly delighted.

"She is well. She writes twice a year," she responded.

"I suppose the letters take a long time to get here?"

"Yes, about four months at least. And mine back to her, the same."

"How long has she left before coming back?"

"About nine years more. It's a very long time."

"Yes, it's a long time."

"And I'm afraid she may not return at all. A lot of convicts find New South Wales to their liking, or they get used to it, and they see ways to make something of themselves out there, which they couldn't do in England, and some marry even while still serving their sentences, and stay there."

"I have heard of a young woman who was sent there for stealing something trivial. She married a man who became an important official, and she returned to England with him in his official capacity. They attended fine dinners, met dignitaries, and crowed over all those who had put her away," Alex said.

This made Tess laugh. Alex laughed too.

How easily they conversed together! No words of love were ever spoken between them. Alex learned that it would be two years before she could apply for her ecclesiastical annulment. She would have to be patient, and in the meantime, she hoped that she was safe from Mrs. Bailey's schemes.

"I wish we could find who had my mother put away," she said then, not laughing anymore.

She told him the entire story of what had happened. He was a good listener.

CHAPTER 52

TALL, THIN WITH A HIGH HAT

"We are going away," Clarence said to his wife abruptly one morning when they passed each other in the hallway. It was the first time she had been addressed by him in weeks. His words shocked her.

"I am not going away," Tess responded.

"You are. You're my wife. I'm going abroad, and you're coming with me."

'Why do not you go alone? Why do I have to come with you? You know we're married in name only. That is your wish as well as mine."

"Perhaps my wishes have altered."

Tess asked Annie to get her shawl, and she set out for a long walk. Her mind was a maelstrom of emotion and confusion. Before she knew it, she walked at a run. She became breathless and stopped outside the Reginald Inn, now the Reginald Hotel, leaning for a moment against the wall there. A carriage passed in the gate and halted at the front entrance. She saw a young man disembark, but there was nothing remarkable about him, until he handed out an older woman who looked about her, evidently pleased with what she saw.

She recognised her instantly. The tall, thin figure, the dark eyebrows under the high, fine hat bedecked with all kinds of decoration, the thin line of her mouth, and the way she carried herself. She was expensively dressed, like a woman of fortune.

Miss Deuville!

Now a young woman disembarked, and she, too, looked familiar, but it was harder to place her. But when she too looked about her, and Tess had a clear view of her face, she saw Stella Hobbs. Her illuminated face on the staircase was imprinted in her mind.

Miss Deuville and Stella Hobbs. What was their connection? Who was the man? Her sweetheart, or husband now perhaps, who had worked at Baddelley Hall?

Her accomplice!

She could hardly catch her breath, yet she knew she did not wish to be seen by them. Although they might not recognise her, as she had been a child then and looked very different, she did not want to take any chances. She hurried back to the house.

Alexander! She had to see him. Her own troubles, that of being taken abroad, had to wait.

She found him in the billiard room practicing shots, and he was by himself. He put down his cue when she hurried in, breathless.

"What is the matter, Tess?"

She told him.

"What shall I do? Do you know what is the best thing to do?" she asked him. "That woman was my mother's enemy, and perhaps Stella Hobbs was sent by her to our home. I cannot let them leave without doing something. My mother is innocent. They had her put away!"

"Calm yourself, Tess. I will do what I can, I promise."

Alexander was in a dilemma. His brother's wife needed help, and his brother would be of no assistance whatsoever. He could not allow these criminals, if that is what they were, to move on without any action on his part to secure justice for Tess' mother.

Alexander did not know what he could do, but as he practiced his break shots, an idea came to him.

CHAPTER 53

ALEX GOES A-COURTING

"I shall not be in for dinner," Alexander announced at lunchtime. He often rode or walked about the country to see his friends, and everybody supposed that he had been engaged to dine with one of them that evening.

"We're to start the shearing in two days," his father said, reminding him that his free time would be limited.

The foyer of the hotel was busy when Alexander walked in that evening. He was carefully dressed, his hair was oiled with macassar, and a scent of cologne drifted about his person.

"Mr. Bailey, sir," the concierge practically bowed to the floor. The first family in the area did not grace his hotel as often as he wished. But here was Mr. Bailey, heir to Stagtarn!

"I would like a dry sherry, please," he said, seating himself by the window, all the better to see everybody coming and going.

A middle aged woman passed by with a girl about thirteen years old. That was not them.

A family with three boys passed. No.

Then a middle-aged woman, tall and thin, dark haired under her stylish hat and walking with great dignity, passed in. She was accompanied by a good-looking woman in her twenties, who looked about her freely, and a young man such as Tess had described. The trio went upstairs and then returned to the dining room for dinner.

"I should like to have dinner here," he said to Mr. Newman, the proprietor. "And I wonder if you could do me a little favour. I should very much like to be introduced to the party who just went into the dining room."

"Very good, sir. A very nice family, sir. All the way from St Albans. Come this way."

He was introduced, and when they realised he was alone, he was invited to dine with them. The older woman was Miss Edith Henry, the younger her niece, Miss Louise Dobbs, and the man was her brother, Mr. Frederick Dobbs.

Not the same names, but never mind.

He singled Miss Dobbs out frequently in the conversation, and before long, Miss Henry was of the opinion that her niece had made a conquest. Later, she made enquiries. Mr. Bailey was heir to much of the land between Stagtarn and Windermere, was very wealthy, and of course, most importantly of all, single.

Mr. Alexander had proposed a Sunday picnic at a very nice spot nearby, and they had been very happy to accept.

CHAPTER 54

AUNT MYRTLE'S PLAN

"He would be a great catch, Stella," Aunt Myrtle said in the room a little later. "Quite frankly, I am tired of going about all over the place."

"As I am, Aunt. But who shall I say I am?"

"Your father was in the Foreign Service and killed. Your mother died of a tropical disease. You, poor little infant, were sent home to my care."

"And who are you, Aunt?"

"This time, I'm the daughter of a bishop. Bishop Henry of St. Albans. I may have to take on that persona permanently."

"But let me keep the name Edward. I keep forgetting who I'm supposed to be," Frederick said.

"We've introduced you as Frederick, so we'll have to keep it at that."

"We'll have to linger here longer than a fortnight, I think." Stella said.

"What? Can't you captivate Mr. Bailey in that time?" Edward asked.

"We shall be prepared to stay the entire summer, if necessary," said her aunt.

"We shouldn't stay here for long, Aunt, it's really not safe." Frederick, aka Edward said.

"We shall depend upon you to become engaged to him sooner rather than later, Stella. Do whatever is necessary. Catch him. In the meantime, it will be nice to stay in a good place such as this is."

"There was that woman gaping at us today when we arrived." Edward said.

"She probably had never seen a good crinoline before in a hole in the wall like this. You had better not wear that brooch, Stella. It's engraved at the back, you know. If you should drop it...the York people had very nice things. I love my pearls. You have good taste, Edward."

"I hope we never have to do this again, though. I'm quite tired of going to new positions and scrubbing the floors of someone who is going to be our victim." Stella said.

"Do not say victim," both said together.

"I, for one, want to stop," she complained. "This is not a natural life. I want to marry somebody and settle down." She paused. "I want to marry Mr. Alexander Bailey."

CHAPTER 55

THE GANG

Alex did not know what to do next, apart from gaining the confidence of the trio by pretending a romantic interest in Louise Dobbs, if that was her name. An invitation to dinner perhaps, a game of billiards with Mr. Dobbs, or get him drunk to find out more about the family? He was too much of a gentleman to get Miss Dobbs tipsy with all that might evolve from that.

Eventually, he simply decided to get the advice of the police, for he was no sleuth, so two days later he and Tess, who needed to come along, and it was quite respectable for a brother-in-law to accompany his sister-in-law on family business, drove in the carriage to Carlisle and visited the police station.

There, with tears at the memory of all she had gone through, Tess began to tell her story. To her surprise, the sergeant took the matter seriously and called a detective from upstairs. He introduced himself as Detective Lang and brought them to his office, and again, Tess poured out the story while he listened attentively.

"This is very useful information," said he after a while. He went to a filing cabinet and took out a thick folder and thumbed through it.

"We are on the lookout for a gang of thieves. A young man and woman. And a third person, possibly an older woman, tall, thin person. What you have told me is a familiar story."

"How?" exclaimed Tess.

"The first crime that we know of began four years ago in Liverpool. A young man got a position of footman in a wealthy household in Knotty Ash. One morning, an emerald tiara and some items of lesser value were missed. Some of the latter were found in another house in Liverpool after a tip-off by their servant, a young woman of good appearance, who reported that she was worried that her mistress was a thief and stealing from the house where she was visiting to give dancing lessons. A search ensued in the dancing teacher's home, some items were found, and she was arrested. The servant disappeared, and a few weeks later, the footman handed in his notice, got a good reference, and left also. Nothing suspicious there about the footman or the girl, at that time."

"Did they recover the emerald tiara?" Alex asked.

"Not recovered, nor were some other items of jewellery. It was assumed the dancing teacher had passed them on to somebody else. She was convicted and sent to Botany Bay for fourteen years for the theft. She strongly protested her innocence even as she was being led onto the ship."

"That is exactly what happened to my mother!" Tess cried, while the detective turned the pages in the folder. "As I was saying, she went to the Baddelleys to make costumes for a wedding and she -"

"Let us listen," Alex said to her gently as the detective began to talk again. Alex ached to take her trembling hand, but he could not.

"Then there was another incident, very like that, in York this time. It was about eighteen months later. There was a young constable there who recognised that something very similar had happened in Liverpool when he had been posted there. The person arrested was a regular visitor to the wealthy household. This time, it was an insurance agent making a series of visits to assess the value of certain items. His woman servant, a young woman of good appearance, having tipped off the police, disappeared in the wake of the person being arrested. The similarity was enough to put us on the alert, and notices were posted out to every police station in the north. And, it happened again, over a year later, in Doncaster. One of the victims saw the girl subsequently in the company of an older woman at the races, tall, thin, and dark, but by the time she had alerted the constable, they had gone."

"It all sounds a bit confusing," Alexander said, frowning.

"This is the way they operate. First, the man answers a genuine advertisement in the newspaper for a wealthy family seeking a manservant. He always has good references. He bides his time there, often for a year or more, until a suitable victim presents himself, the dancing teacher, the agent, and in the latest case, in Doncaster, the governess who lived out. The person has to live out and have a servant. When he chooses his victim, he tells his female accomplice to entice the victim's servant away with a good sum of money and present herself in her place, having 'heard' they were in need of a servant. She also has good references.

"Within a short time, there is a theft at the rich house. One or two items of great value, and smaller items to frame the hapless victim. The footman hands over these to the girl, who plants them on her master or mistress, and then makes a complaint to the police that she thinks her mistress is stealing from her employer. Meantime, the theft at the wealthy home is discovered. A search ensues, following on from the complaint from the girl. The most expensive items are never recovered, and it is assumed that this is passed on to the older woman, who is also in the locality, and sold by her to enable them to live in style until it is time for the next crime."

"We thought that Miss Deuville was taking revenge on my mother," Tess said.

"From what you have told me, that was the most likely motive, and this worked so well for them that they decided to repeat it, this time for sheer greed."

"We knew there was a connection between Stella and the footman at Baddelley Hall. We thought they were sweethearts, but if the family at the Reginald are this gang, they are sister and brother."

"In all of the other cases, no connection was suspected between the footman and the victim's servant," Detective Lang said. "They fine-tuned the crime."

"Will my mother be allowed to come home, then?" Tess asked, her clasped hands against her breast.

"I cannot promise you the outcome of any investigation," Detective Lang said. He turned to Alexander. "Tell me more about this party staying at the hotel at Stagtarn."

As they left, the detective watched them out the window. Mrs. Clarence Bailey stumbled on the steps and Mr. Alexander instantly put out a hand to steady her, and it seemed to the detective that the hand lingered upon her back longer than it should have. The look he gave her was that of great solicitation.

"Hmmm," he mumbled to himself.

"What wheels are turnin' in your mind?" asked Detective Fenwick, amused.

"There's an unsolved murder in Stagtarn." Lang said. "We have statements from a dozen people who said they saw Mr. Alexander Bailey, and the witness at the scene of the crime who said it was not him, and I wonder if she was lying. It is a very puzzling case."

CHAPTER 56

VINDICATION!

The party at Stagtarn were making themselves ready to go out to drive to Lake Windermere when a knock came to their doors. There was a dead silence at first when the police entered both rooms. Stella looked terrified.

They were told to sit down while the rooms were searched. The police found a great deal of expensive jewellery. Stella began to sob. Aunt Myrtle was stony-faced. In the room next door, Edward said nothing. They were all arrested.

A crowd gathered to see the spectacle, in spite of the proprietor, Mr. Newman, pleading with them to go away and mind their own business.

"How did you find us?" Aunt asked coldly as they were put into the police van.

"You were recognised."

"Recognised? By whom?"

"By a young woman whose mother you sent down for fourteen years. Her name was Miss Tess Woods then, and she lived in Preston. She saw you when you were arriving. She and her brother-in-law came to see me yesterday. He is Mr. Alexander Bailey."

"Mr. Bailey! She sent him to look us out!" sobbed Stella. "Oh, what treachery!"

"I knew she looked suspicious," Edward said with disgust. "We should have left first thing this morning."

This story caused a sensation in the village and reached Stagtarn Hall at lunchtime. As nobody but Alexander was aware that Tess had any connection with the criminal gang, it was discussed freely. Tess was restless and fidgety.

"Will they be sent to Botany Bay?" was all she asked.

"No, they've stopped sending prisoners there. Botany Bay and Van Diemens are proper countries now, and don't want our criminals." Alexander answered her. “They’re on the up and up.”

Alexander thought it wise to take his father into his confidence about Tess' mother as they worked together with the sheep the following day. The old man was shocked and not at all confident that Tess' mother had been innocent.

Tess went to tell the Stowes that afternoon. She received a cool greeting, as they were still upset that Annie had left them for Tess. They had another girl who was not half as willing or cheerful as Annie had been.

"So that's what all that was about," cried Aunt Belle. "Everybody's talking about it! I wish I'd seen them taken away!"

"Mama can come home!" Tess exulted. "But there has to be a lawyer who will inform the judge, or something! Can you arrange it, Uncle, please?"

They did not wish to be involved there. Money was tight they said, and Mr. Clarence was the proper person to fund a lawyer, not them. He was her husband, after all. She mustn't come to them for help when she was married so well.

CHAPTER 57

THE SHEARING SHED

While Tess was at her uncle's, Clarence waited for his father to go inside before he joined his brother in the shearing shed. The labourers were not within hearing, and the sheep were making a racket in any case, so Clarence felt free to speak. They had not spoken for days.

"What is it?"

"You want everything, don't you?" Clarence said to him, his fist closed.

"I don't know what you're talking about," Alex said, holding the ewe on her back between his knees with one arm, and his shears deftly cutting the wool from her belly with the other.

"You have all this." Clarence swept his arm about in a wide wave. "You have the hall, the farm, all the land, and everything in it, but you're not content, are you?"

"I don't know what you're talking about," Alex said, his anger growing. He stopped shearing, let go of the sheep, and stood up. The half-sheared ewe made a run for freedom.

"You want my wife, don't you?" Clarence said, leaning in to him, his face full of jealous aggression, his fist to his brother's face.

Alex was taken aback. It became clear to him. Clarence had no interest in his wife, but he must have observed them speaking together, and of course there was that excursion to Carlisle which he was not at liberty to explain. Tess, too, was not discreet enough, nor perhaps wise enough, to hide her preference. Clarence had become jealous.

"You're not having her," Clarence said with triumph. "She's mine. Where were you on Tuesday? What business could she possibly have in Carlisle that she needed to go there? Have you cuckolded me?"

"I have not. How dare you suggest it." Alex said angrily. "I don't know why you hate me so much. Just because I didn't die to allow you all this." He swept his arm about in imitation of his brother's gesture earlier. "Just because you didn't succeed in having me hanged. If you put a hand on me, I will defend myself to the death, and I will be acquitted."

Alexander was trembling with fury. Without being aware of it, he brandished the shearing blade.

His brother's face lost its hardness. He loosened his fist and looked down.

"I wouldn't have been happy at that. No, thinking about it later, I was glad. I am sorry I agreed to it. No, no, don't say anything about my mother. It's her life's work to get this land back into her family. I think it's making her a little unbalanced, to be honest. I have to try to get out from under her influence. I know it's very meager to say it, but I am sorry. Very."

"There is some fraternal feeling then, Cain." Alex threw the shears upon the ground.

"Cain and Abel. Yes, that's who we are. You can have everything. It's all your birthright, but my wife is mine. You leave my wife alone." Clarence remembered his original intention in seeking out his brother.

Alex said nothing.

"Did you not hear me, Alexander? *Thou shalt not covet thy brother's wife.*"

He left. Alexander was furious and went in search of the errant sheep, and giving up, went to his father who had announced his intention of checking the sheepfold near the stream.

Ephraim Bailey kept his sons on a tight rein economically. They had allowances, but Alex had nothing to hand that would set in motion a speedy pardon for Mrs. Woods and to have her returned to Tess. At it's very fastest, it would take a year, as messages to the other side of the world took several months.

Alex found his father crouched down by the sheepfold. His rugged face had an annoyed look when he saw his son.

"Have you seen this? Two big stones over with the last wind, and nobody told me. An invitation to Mr. Fox. It's a miracle he hasn't found it yet. I have to have a word with Smith. He should look to the shepherds, as they're lazy. What's the point of having an agent, and why don't you see these things, Alex? What do you want?"

"Nothing, Father." His father was in a foul mood, and he felt it best to drop the subject of funds.

"Yes, you do, I know you do. And I think I know what it is. Let me tell you Alex, you have far too much interest in the affairs of a certain lady, if lady she be. Your brother's wife. Leave her alone. Leave them alone. I'm not shelling out for a lawyer to get her mother pardoned. Don't even ask me, Alexander. It's more in your line to get yourself a wife. Come on, come on, help me put these two stones back."

The conversation was over before it even had happened, and as Alex bent and helped to wedge the stones back into place, he knew all was lost before it began.

He could not face Tess that evening at dinner, so he went out to the hotel again. In walking home, he thought deeply about all that Clarence, and his father, had said to him. There was only one course open to him. He had to put a distance between him and his brother's wife.

I almost wish she'd named me as the murderer, was his unbidden and unbalanced thought. *My brother doesn't love her. I do.*

CHAPTER 58

A DREADFUL TURN OF EVENTS

He's avoiding me, Tess thought, when Alex appeared and disappeared quickly over the next weeks without as much as a nod in her direction.

Now that Tess was confident that her husband had no interest in her, Annie was given her own bed in the attics like the other servants. She was unhappy. The others were clannish and did not welcome her. The Stowes had asked her to return to them and she had agreed, for she was so used to them, to their house, and to their ways that every other place felt like a foreign land. They promised a fire in her room and a bigger wage. Tess understood, but she felt lonely now.

Then Alexander went away and stayed away. What could she do about her mother's case when he was not here? He seemed to have abandoned her. She could, she supposed, write to the police in Preston. With this in mind, she climbed the stairs to her room that night, resolving to do it first thing in the morning. Jane, the housemaid, helped her into her nightgown and tucked her in. It was the way of the wealthy, even if she felt it was ridiculous.

She had blown out the candle and was falling asleep when her door opened, and Clarence came in with a light. He was dressed in only his nightshirt.

"What do you want?" she asked him, half-sitting up, frightened.

"I want my marital rights," he said.

"Go away!" she cried.

"You can't refuse me. You must submit to me. Don't you understand?"

"I thought we were to get an annulment, and this would make it far more difficult!" she pulled the sheet up to her chin.

"Who said anything about an annulment? I want you. Only you." The candle near his face showed a leering grin.

"It's your duty, Mrs. Clarence," he said.

She looked at him, aghast. The candle was set on the bedside table. He got in beside her and blew the candle out. The harvest moon shone in through a crack in the curtains.

. . .

The following morning, she felt as if her world had ended. With the consummation of her marriage, her hope was gone. She despised them all, her parents-in-law, her husband, the Stowes. Even Alex, who had deserted her when she most needed him. He did not return from his friend's home, and nobody seemed to know where he was, or else they would not say so, before her.

The weeks and months wore on, and Clarence came to her several times a week. She could not refuse him, as he was her husband. Sometimes he just wished to talk, and he wanted her to listen to him. His childhood. How he might have been fond of Alex but had not been allowed. How his mother was obsessed with the Livingstone land and that he was beginning to think the effort a great waste of time and energy. How he was glad that Alexander had not been arrested. And then, how glad he was that she had become his wife, for she was a nice, good person, and he liked her eyes, and her skin had become uncommonly good. Maybe he would be a better person with her by his side.

Clarence, to Tess, began to seem like a human being, albeit a very wayward, criminal human being. She was always afraid of him and relieved when she had the bedchamber to herself.

Christmas was upon them. The house was decorated. How she hated Christmas! How many years now since her mother had been taken from her? She had lost count! Every Christmas brought the memories back, especially the popular carol *'Deck the Halls'*. Why was she always hearing *'Deck the Halls'*? The governess had taught it to the children, and they sang it everywhere.

On Christmas morning, she had to face another trial. She had been sick every morning for weeks, unable to face breakfast. Her breakfast that morning, brought to her room on a tray, was returned without being touched.

Mrs. Bailey came to tell her what the matter was.

"You're with child," she said. "A child with Livingstone blood!"

"Oh no, no, no!" she said after her mother in law had left the room. She put her head in her hands. "Oh, now I will be tied to him forever! This is the worst news I could get, a Christmas gift I do not want. Another horrid Christmas. Why does Christmas never bring me joy?"

CHAPTER 59

BOXING DAY

Alex returned that day, but only for a brief visit. He received the news from his delighted half-brother Clarence.

"The summer. It'll be the summer, Mother says. Oh, and I misjudged you, Alex. You didn't cuckold me. She was a virgin. And she came to me so willingly."

"Shut up!" Alex could hardly contain his temper at Clarence speaking thus of his own wife. The news had shattered him. The thought of Clarence and Tess spending nights together affected him in a way he did not expect. He avoided her. It upset him deeply to see her as she was, a wife and soon-to-be-mother. He also could not avoid asking himself the question if she was falling in love with Clarence. '*She came to me.* Did Clarence mean that she instigated the intimacy? If he had stayed, would everything have stayed the way it had been? He felt confused, sad, hurt, and angry all at once. Perhaps Tess had decided to make the best of the situation. Who could blame her for that? But his own hopes were dashed.

Tess saw the avoidance. She understood it. But she was Clarence's wife. There was no help for that. She felt trapped, resentful, and very sad.

It was a tense Christmas Day. Alexander and Clarence could hardly bear to be in the same room, and they never spoke. The Christmas spirit was absent from Stagtarn Hall. Tess was glad to climb the stairs to her bedchamber. She hoped to be alone tonight, and Clarence did not come. He was to be up early tomorrow for the foxhunt.

The following morning Tess woke to the sounds of the hunting horn and the excited baying of dogs, as horses and humans added their own sounds while the hunt assembled. The hunt would proceed to the village and go through it; it was a tradition. In other years, her uncle's public house was filled with revellers, and the ladies of the hunt retired to the back parlour, where they were brought drinks, tea, and sandwiches. That was where Mrs. Bailey and her girls were, for the governess was on holiday. They had left Tess out of the arrangements for the day, but she was glad not to be in their company, though the girls had become more friendly to her. The youngest, Lily, was a sweet child who needed love and sought her out frequently, for her mother was not affectionate toward her youngest.

She could have walked to her uncle's and helped him as in previous years, but she felt it would be frowned upon by her new family. In any case, the crowds there might make her feel ill. She looked forward to a quiet day in the house, as all the gentlemen were at the hunt. She went for a bracing walk and returned to sit by the blazing fire in the drawing room.

She was surprised to see her brother-in-law seated there with magazines and newspapers by him.

"Alex!" she said, in surprise. "Why aren't you at the foxhunt?"

"I have no horse," he said.

"Where is she? Where is Gaia?"

"I sold her." His tone was a little distant.

"And you didn't buy another?"

"No, not yet. I trust you are well?" He managed a polite smile.

"I'm well, thank you." She did not miss his tone. "I am not happy, but I am well."

A silence elapsed. The subject uppermost in Tess' mind was that of her mother and the pardon, but she could not ask. He continued to read his *Country Gentleman* magazine. Evidently, he was not in the mood to talk. Everything now was altered between them. She was not a wife in name only anymore, and she was starting a family.

She took up *Follets,* a favourite of all fashionable women, and browsed the lavish fashion plates, pondering the particulars of how each garment was sewn.

Finally, Alex put down his magazine.

"I cannot sit here with you and not talk," he said. "I have news for you."

She looked up in hope.

"I have been in contact with a barrister, a Mr. Gregory, about your mother's case," he said. "They are very hopeful of getting the matter resolved within three months, and then word can be sent to Australia, and your mother can come home."

"Alex! Oh, Alex! Thank you!" Her eyes were shining with happy tears.

"She may be with you in about fifteen months or so." His eyes were lit up at her pleasure and gratitude, but they hid his broken heart.

"Oh, your dear father! He is a generous man!"

"Do not mention it to him, I pray you. He is very prickly upon matters such as these. Not a word, please, to Father."

"Are you sure? I will not mention it then."

Tess did not feel like sitting anymore. She wanted to dance!

"I thought you had forgotten all about it," she said on impulse, flinging down the magazine and walking about the room.

"No! I did not forget." He took up his magazine again and said no more.

Tess hardly minded. His news was uppermost in his mind. She was jubilant that her mother's case was reopened. The New Year came in, she began to feel better and able to eat again, and slowly began to accept the new life growing in her.

CHAPTER 60

POLICE VISIT

On the 2nd day of the New Year, Alexander was preparing to leave again. His father had given him a great deal of trouble about selling his horse, which haranguing he had borne with fortitude. He would not tell his father why he had parted with such a fine mare. Barristers did not come cheap. He was getting ready to walk to the village to procure a horse to take him back to Windermere.

There was a knock at the front door, and the butler, Mr. Grogan, was very surprised to see two policemen standing there.

"Is Mr. Alexander Bailey here, please? We'd like a word with him."

Tess was looking over the balcony in the Hall. She was dumbfounded. What did the constables want with Alexander? Was it something about her mother? She came downstairs.

Alex was summoned and went into the drawing room. Jane, the housemaid, was in there already, and before she was observed by Detective Lang, he had said, "Mr. Alexander Bailey, if you don't mind sir, we'd just like to hear again of your whereabouts on the day Mr. Reginald Turnbull was murdered. That is, the 15th day of March last year."

"Well, of course, please be seated gentlemen. Jane, that will do for now. You may go."

"Yes, sir." Jane gathered up her dusters very quickly.

"Of course, I understand completely." Alexander patiently began to list his movements of that afternoon, beginning with eating luncheon with his stepmother.

When Jane left the room, she almost knocked over Tess, who was approaching the door of the drawing room, wondering if she dared to go in.

"Oh, I'm sorry, Mrs. Clarence! They're askin' 'im about the murder!" Jane was distraught. "And he didn't do it."

"No, of course not."

Jane hurried to the kitchen, where she dropped her dusters and got her cloak from a nail in the back hall.

"Where are you going?" asked the housekeeper, who had seen her dash.

Jane did not reply. She ran as fast as she dared over the icy yard, past the outhouses, to the stables.

"They're going to take him! They're going to take Mr. Alexander! Where's my father? He has to speak now!"

CHAPTER 61

THE GROOMSMAN SPEAKS

The drawing room door was opened, and the butler entered the room, accompanied by an old groomsman in worsted jacket and trousers, and Jane, the housemaid, still wrapped in her cloak. He coughed to get attention.

"What is it?" asked Alexander.

"If I might interrupt your discourse, gentlemen, this is Joseph Ball. He is groomsman here, and this is his daughter Jane. Joe has something to tell you about the day Mr. Turnbull was murdered. It should have been told to you long before this, but it was not, and better late than never I suppose." He cast a reproachful eye upon the groomsman.

"Nobody ever asked me," Joe said indignantly. "If they had, I would've told them."

"Do you have any information?" asked the constable

"I do indeed, sir. That afternoon, Mrs. Bailey gave us all time off. All the boys went down the village, on various errands or amusements, but I did not. I was feeling poorly with my rheumatism, and I went to my bed, which is in the coach house. My daughter Jane, who is housemaid here, gave me a cordial and a rub of liniment, and she was still there when the stable door opened."

"Yes?" The policemen were very interested.

"I heard footsteps coming in. As the mistress had given us the afternoon off, I did not want whoever it was to know I was there in case I was asked to do a job, like, so I stayed quiet as a mouse, and when Jane saw who it was, she didn't need no tellin' to hide, but that's another story."

Jane looked down at the carpet and bit her lip.

"I saw Mr. Clarence come into the stable," continued the old man. "I expected him to go and get his own horse, Nelson, but he did not. Instead, he went to his brother's horse, Gaia, the dappled grey mare. I was surprised, but again, did not say a word. There was nothin' wrong with Nelson that I knew that he should've got a loan of Gaia.

"Then there was a bit of commotion. Gaia is a very uneasy horse, and she knew it wasn't Mr. Alexander or me or any of the lads who was saddlin' her up, and she got a bit restless, like, and when he mounted 'er, she reared a bit. And he shouted to her angrily. Now I never heard Alexander address any beast like that in my life, and I knows him from a lad. He started shouting cos she wasn't moving an inch, and the more he shouted, the more nervous Gaia got, and he got his crop and whipped her. And that did it. She threw him. Into the straw. He got up, brushed himself down, and then began to talk more calm to her, like, and rub her. And she calmed down, and after a while he mounted again, and they were off."

"Are you certain it was Mr. Clarence?"

"Yes, for I saw his face clearly. And when he fell into the straw, his hat come off and the muffler came undone. Jane knew it was 'im from the get-go."

"His walk, his voice, his face, everything." Jane ventured. "I'd swear in a court of law to that."

While Joseph has giving his statement, Mrs. Bailey had come downstairs and into the room. She began to shout at Joe, calling him a liar. Then Clarence appeared.

"It's no use, Mother," he said wearily. "Joe is correct." He turned to the constables. "It was I who was on Gaia that afternoon. I shot Mr. Turnbull and tried to make it look as if my brother did it."

"No, no! He is raving! I tell you!" Mrs. Bailey screamed. By now all the servants were gathered outside the door.

"No, I am not raving, Mother. I'm tired of the burden. I killed a man and tried to make it look as if my brother did it. I can't carry the burden anymore. What a relief, to have it out in the open. I am a murderer! I'm Cain, and I tried to kill my brother!" He shouted the last two sentences.

He made no protest as he was arrested and handcuffed.

"You may say goodbye to your wife," the policeman said.

"Goodbye, wife. I hope our child is everything his father is not."

"Clarence, I'll pray for you." Tess was near to tears. There was more depth and feeling to her husband than she had thought. She had glimpsed his repentant, tortured soul. She meant what she said. She was carrying his child, and she would pray for him. She did not love him, but he had unburdened himself to her, and she regretted that a child, who might have been good and generous, had been trained up to be greedy to the point of murder to get what he wanted.

Her child would grow up without his father, and how would she explain to him why?

"Be good to them," is the only other thing he said as he was being led out. He said it to Alexander. His eyes dropped and he pressed his lips together as if not knowing what to respond. He was utterly relieved that Clarence had confessed, but it did not alter how he felt about Tess now.

He still felt distant and awkward, and wondered if she had loved him after all.

Clarence's mother tried to embrace him. He did not look at her and said nothing.

CHAPTER 62

SENTENCED

Mr. Bailey had been sent for, and when he came in, Clarence had already been taken away. He dropped into a chair and became ill. He could not move one side of his body, and his speech was slurred. One side of his face drooped.

The doctor was summoned, and he was diagnosed with an apoplectic seizure.

Soon it became evident that he would not recover, and that it was only a matter of days before he would slip away.

The house became very quiet and sorrowful. Ephraim's daughters came and hugged him one last time, weeping. He was older than most fathers, but he loved them, and they had always felt it. He died in the middle of January and was buried on a hilly churchyard overlooking the lake, where all the Baileys had been laid to rest. His widow was sorrowful and bitter, for there was nothing she could do now. Her work of nearly twenty years had come to nothing. Word was sent to Carlisle jail where Clarence was being held pending the spring assizes.

For several days, the girls were inconsolable at the loss of their father. Tess had several months ago begun to help them with their seams, samplers, and embroidery, and so they had begun to know and like each other. She had become quite a favourite.

Clarence's sisters were not aware of the very serious charge against their brother. It had been kept from them. There was no need to impart bad news before it was absolutely necessary.

Mrs. Bailey herself was suddenly attentive to Tess.

"I have something to say to you." she said to her. "I have a very good expectation that Clary will be acquitted, for a jury will not believe a stableman whose eyesight is not what it was, nor his unintelligent daughter. They will be destroyed during cross-examination, and I have engaged the best barrister in England. I hope that Alexander will be generous and give Clary half of everything. He will need it, with you and a child. You should petition Alex about it, very strongly."

"You forget that Clarence admitted the murder," Tess said.

"That was in the heat of the moment, and not admissible, I am sure."

Tess made no further comment.

Spring came in, and the countryside bloomed. The assizes took place. Tess did not go. Her mother-in-law attended.

Clarence pleaded guilty and did not ask for mercy. The victim's brothers wanted 'a life for a life' and the judge sentenced him to death. Tess received the news that evening from Alexander, who returned from the court alone. He and his stepmother had gone separately and would return in the same way.

"How is your stepmother?" Tess asked him.

"Distraught."

"Will she have to leave here?"

Alex put down his glass.

"I do not want her here," he said flatly. "I wanted to eject her after my father died, but for my sisters' sake, I postponed it."

"Are you going to throw her out now?"

"Do I not have good reason?" He sounded a little irritated.

"Yes, you do." Tess said quietly. "Of course, you do."

"She has an ample jointure from my father. She and the girls will take a house, perhaps move back to the house she grew up in. Do you know it? Beckley House. It's only a mile off."

"I know it. Nobody lives there now since her father died. You will be here alone, then. For I must go too. I will be her son's widow."

"Yes, you must go too." He seemed very definite about that.

"The girls. Do they know yet about Clarence?"

He shook his head.

"Oh, I will have to tell them," Tess said, putting down her work.

"Will you? I would be happy to be spared the task."

"It's my place," she said. "My husband, and their brother."

She mounted the stairs to the classroom. There, with the governess present, she told Maria, Grace, and Lily about Clarence. The tears were instant, loud, and many. The screams resonated throughout the large house. Tess gathered them about her and embraced them.

Alexander heard the screams. He went out for a long, long walk to Thora Tarn and did not return for dinner. Mrs. Bailey returned angry, would speak to nobody, and went straight to bed. Tess ate in the large dining room alone, for the older girls, Maria and Grace, who usually dined with the family now, had been given a sedative and put to bed by their governess. Lily had cried herself to sleep.

Night fell and the candles were lit.

What was her future to be like?

CHAPTER 63

A DREADFUL SPECTACLE

It was a public hanging, and thousands of people gathered to see 'the gentleman' drop to his death at the end of a rope. Men estimated the height of the prisoner and betted upon the drop, which would be stated in the broadsheets the following day. Women held their babies in their arms and talked excitedly about the coming spectacle to their older children. The hanging was the talk of the district and beyond, reaching over the border to Scotland.

Mrs. Bailey had stayed at home and could not face the spectacle, and Tess did not want to go into a crowd of cheering people with more of a lust for sensation than for justice. However, as Clarence's wife, she felt it her duty to visit him in the condemned cell in the County Cumberland Prison the evening before.

"I deserve what I'm getting," he said matter-of-factly. "If I'd been brought up differently, I wouldn't be here. But I wasn't. Look out for her, will you? And the girls? You're stronger in your mind that I thought you were. I got very fond of you, Tess. We could have been happy, couldn't we?"

Tess privately doubted that, but she took his hands and told him that she would look after his mother and his sisters and pray for his soul.

"Will you stay until tomorrow, and be there? I want to be able to see you before they put the hood on. I've asked the chaplain if he will look after you."

She agreed reluctantly. The chaplain had arranged a room for her in a boarding house very close to the jail. The bed was uncomfortable, and from dawn onwards she was disturbed by noise outside.

The streets were already crowding with people from the towns and the villages, even from over the border. There was a sound of revelry. She woke early and went to the jail, and with the courteous assistance of an official, was afforded a seat at the dreaded location. The awful scaffold was before her; she was only feet away from the wood. The burgeoning crowds were held back by several barricades which strained with the pressure of bodies. The crowd was excited and chattering, and shouts of impatience erupted as the time for the execution neared. The windows were filled with curious faces. Boys and young men climbed any part of a building they could hang on to. There were costermongers selling hot buns and cakes. There were printer's boys selling accounts of the murder. It was disgusting to rejoice so at the death of anybody, even a murderer.

There was a cheer and a ripple of excitement in the throng when a man mounted the scaffold. Apparently, everybody knew who he was. The hangman, all the way from London! He inspected the work done by the carpenters and checked the rope for stability. The benches near Tess began to fill with minor officials belonging to the judiciary and the prison. They did not share the revelry of the crowd. The gravity of the occasion was reflected on every face.

Then the prison door opened and Clarence, his arms pinioned, was led out. He was preceded by a chaplain who held the Bible and prayed aloud the 90th Psalm. Clarence's terrified eyes immediately sought hers. He ascended the awful steps, and she saw his eyes fill with tears. She wondered if he had seen her put her hand impulsively on her heart. She did not love him, but she trembled for him just the same, and she felt the exulting noises all around must surely be revolting to God. This is a human being, she wanted to shout to them.

The chaplain accompanied him to the last step and the white hood was put over his head. He shivered violently and the chaplain put out his hand to his shoulder. Tess was close enough to see that, before his face was covered, his mouth had trembled in weeping. He mumbled something. Was it her name? She saw the convulsions of his sobbing face through the cotton as the hangman reached for the dreaded bolt to open the trapdoor.

"I'm here! I'm here!" she called out, without knowing she did so.

Oh, God, have mercy on his soul! The plea ascended from the bottom of her heart.

A long groan came from the assembled throng as he dropped. Tess could not look directly. This was the most dreadful scene she had ever witnessed in her life. She put her hand on her stomach as if to protect her child from the spectacle, as well as herself. It was a horrible sight, a public hanging! Satisfied, the crowd began to disperse, leaving a great mess of litter blowing about after them.

"Justice is done!" A gathering of men was in front of the barrier. Tess hadn't noticed them before. "Justice for our poor brother!"

They were Mr. Turnbull's relatives.

Tess arrived home several hours later to find that Alexander had been there and departed again.

"Alexander has told us to leave within the week," Mrs. Bailey said in a sulky monotone. "Where are we to go? What are we to do? This is my home. This is the

Livingstone home, and he does not have one drop of Livingstone blood."

Does she not know her son was hanged just a few hours ago? Tess asked herself. *Is it possible that she has blocked it out? I had better not tell her that I was there. All her energy, all her love for life, has gone.*

But she was wrong, for in the next sentence, Mrs. Bailey said, "All I have to look forward to now is my poor son's child. It will be a boy, I know. He must be named Clarence Livingstone Bailey."

Suddenly Tess saw that all her failed ambition for her son would now be transferred to her grandson. She had to nip that in the bud. Immediately!

"If it is a boy, I am calling him after my father Michael Patrick," she said firmly.

"Michael Patrick!" Mrs. Bailey's tone was one of disgust. She flounced about the room. "Everybody is against me. I might as well be dead. I wish I were dead." She burst into a fit of weeping, stopping only to accuse Tess of not having loved Clarence. Tess did not want to discuss or argue anything with her. She too felt distressed and exhausted, and she left the room.

Maria, Grace, and Lily found her and gathered about her. They seemed to look to her to be strong. No words needed to be said; there was no need to describe the awful event to them. All she said was, "Clarence is gone into eternity; he had the chaplain, and God's mercy." They had questions.

"Was it quick? Did it hurt him?"

"It was very quick, and hurt him not at all." Tess tried not to think about those fearful minutes until his body was still. She'd opened her eyes to see him and wished she had not.

"Where is he to be buried?"

"He has already been buried in the prison cemetery." They did not like this.

"Why did he kill Mr. Turnbull, Tess? "Was Mr. Turnbull a very bad man?" The questions got harder and harder. She managed to answer them.

Ephraim had left Clarence five thousand pounds, which would belong to Tess as soon as the will was probated. Mrs. Bailey was quite angry at this. Though she had been generously provided for, she would have liked control over Clarence's money, too. But Tess was his widow, and past twenty-one. She could do nothing about it except complain that the world was against her. She formed the impression that Tess had somehow tricked Clarence into marriage in some sort of blackmail arrangement.

This is impossible, Tess thought, as the words hit her ears. *I can't put up with this much longer. She's going insane.*

That her mother-in-law's strong personality would leave a stamp on her grandson or granddaughter was a possibility she did not want to even think about. What was she going to do? She feared this influence over her child after it was born and as he grew. Her mother-in-law was not yet forty years old!

My own Mama will return next year, and she will know what to do. We will make a home together, Mama, the baby and me.

They moved into the home of 'Old Clary' Livingstone, Beckley House. It was about half the size of Stagtarn and had not been inhabited for years now. It was damp and cold. It would need cleaning, fires, and servants. Mrs. Bailey declared herself unable to interview or engage anybody. Tess would have to do it. Tess would have to do everything. There was no money for a housekeeper or a butler. And the governess had to be let go, so the girls were unoccupied, and by turns busy and bored with their own amusements.

Hardly knowing the hows or the wherefores, Tess managed to engage a cook, a kitchen maid, two housemaids and the cook's brother as a manservant. Mrs. Bailey found fault with all of them. She wouldn't have engaged a cook who was as young as Mrs. Hutch. The kitchen maid looked sloppy in appearance. The housemaids had a dishonest look, and the small one was impertinent. And the cook's brother! She was sure he drank.

Tess reminded herself often that her mother was coming home. That thought kept her from losing her mind as she tried to run the chaotic household. The cook only lasted two weeks before leaving in high dudgeon over Mrs. Bailey's continued complaints. The other servants seemed set to go the same way. Mrs. Bailey was herself a good cook, and Tess asked her to please use her skills in the kitchen. Full of offended dignity, she complied. The kitchen maid, however, left the day after she took over, so her older daughters had to help her. There was a great deal of emotion in the kitchen, but Tess closed the doors, and Lily kept to her side in the drawing room. Upstairs, the housemaids were away from her complaints and decided to stay. Tess kept herself busy sewing her layette and wondering why Alex never came to see them.

She could clearly see Stagtarn from the upper windows of the house, and she wondered if he was there.

CHAPTER 64

ALEX HAS DOUBTS

Although in a household with four other females, Tess felt very alone. Responsibilities weighed upon her. She quarreled with her mother-in-law, standing up for herself when criticised. Tess discovered that she had some of her mother's mettle. The woman was so spiritually sick, so unhappy. She never mentioned Clarence, but she had plenty to say of her stepson. She seemed obsessed by him.

"He has all now. Everything he ever wanted. All to himself, mind. I warrant he sits by the fire every evening and laughs at us."

She was wrong. Just a mile up the road, Alex was deeply unhappy and lonely. He loathed the house, with the dark corridors, the gloomy rooms, the long dining room table at which he alone ate, the empty drawing room.

Memories of his stepmother haunted him. A mile away was not far enough away.

It could have been so different, he thought to himself. Clary and I could have been like real brothers, but we were not allowed that.

He had received a broadsheet printed the day after Clarence's execution. It was lavish and lurid in detail, and he had shaken his head in disgust. The writer had described how his widow had been at the scaffold, weeping. She had approached the condemned man and attempted to embrace him, only to be blocked by the constables. She had cried hysterically, according to the writer, and fell down in a faint as he dropped to his death and had to be borne away. The writer described her condition with such pity that Alexander was sure half of Carlisle and Scotland was weeping. There were large illustrations of Mrs. Bailey falling in a dead faint while in the background, the figure of a man hung limply from a rope. Disgusting. He did not believe half of it.

But had she really been there? It troubled him. Had she loved him?

If she had loved him, could he, Alexander, love her?

I must forget her, he thought. For she's inextricably bound to Clarence's mother. She is having Clarence's child. She belongs to them. And the girls, my half-sisters! I have to let them go also. Lily is a sweet little thing, Grace rather serious and sad, and Maria will soon be out in society. But their mother - I never want to see that murderess again. Why did Clarence protect her? She should be where he is now.

In Windermere, he had a friend named George McPherson. He would ask him to visit for a few days and he would ask his advice. George was an estate agent and Alexander had a mind to have Stagtarn evaluated. Perhaps it would lead to a very big decision in his life.

CHAPTER 65

THE FINAL ATTEMPT

Why am I saddled with her? How did this happen? Tess asked herself the question several times a day. There was no peace in the house. They were, of course, grieving. Two close family members had died in a very short time. Or was everybody grieving? She thought that Mrs. Bailey was not grieving so much for her son as for the hope, now dashed once again, of getting the Livingstone land restored.

"I am back where I began," Mrs. Bailey lamented to herself.

She brooded as she cooked, when she was not quarrelling with her two emotional daughters. She brooded as she lay awake at night. The work of twenty years was completely wasted. She had failed. But another door was opening up. *If Alexander were not in the way, everything would fall to*

Maria as next in line. He had hardly made a will. Maria could then marry one of her Livingstone cousins. Again, the prospect of success enticed her forward to think the unthinkable.

But Alexander was like a cat with nine lives!

There has to be a way, she said to herself over and over, getting up one night and pacing her room with the full moon shining in the window. There has to be a way. I was very stupid the first time, as I knew nothing of poisons, and for the second and the third I trusted other people. I will have to do this myself. What would Old Clary do?

CHAPTER 66

AT LAST

It seemed to Lydia that the easiest way was for an accident to happen to him was with a gun, and she was prepared to wield it. She would go to him with a pistol and say that she was going to shoot herself in front of him.

He would attempt to take it away from her, and she'd shoot him. But what if she accidentally shot herself? Could she give her life for the Livingstone land?

No, Lydia, she said to herself. *You will not shoot yourself. You will shoot him. The police will be told that he tried to get the gun from me, and that in doing so it went off, hitting him. I will take my chances with the jury if I am arrested.*

The more she thought about the scheme, the more she liked it. Alexander was a gentleman. She envisaged him walking slowly toward her, speaking gently, his hand out for the gun. As long as she kept the weapon pointing at herself and then turned it upon him at the last moment, then it could be more easily explained as accidental as she could point it upwards as if in a struggle. He was so much taller than she, she could not miss.

She had to go back to Stagtarn, preferably at night when all the servants were in bed. She knew all the entrances and where the spare keys were secreted.

She went that evening, secreting a loaded pistol under her cloak, and let herself in the servant's entrance. Everything was dark, but she knew where the candles and matches were. She lit one to light her way through the back hallway and kitchen. Everybody had gone to bed.

Up the servant staircase and into the connecting door leading to the family part of the house. She saw a light under the drawing room door. She set the candle down on the table outside, and with a firm wrench of her wrist, she turned the doorknob.

There were three people there! Alexander, a man she recognised as his friend McPherson from Windermere, and his brother Percy.

Alexander rose to his feet. "How did you get in?" He never greeted her now as 'Mother.'

There was no going-back. She had to make it look like an accident for the witnesses. She said nothing, just put her hand inside her cloak and drew out the pistol, pointing it at her head.

There was a gasp of horror from the group.

"Don't," Alexander said, rising and advancing toward her as she knew he would.

"I have nothing left. My son is gone. My land is gone. I have nothing left."

Alex looked at her for a long moment. "Wait," he said. "I cannot bring Clarence back to you, but if you want the land, you can have it."

He sat down again and looked at her with expectation.

His companions looked at him in amazement.

"I can have it?" She looked at him, her eyes mocking.

"Yes, you can have it all, and this house too, for I hate it. When I was a boy confined to my room upstairs, with no company except Nurse Wren and a few books, I wanted a big adventure. I never wanted all this, but I did not want to upset Father. He loved the land so much, he would have been aghast that I did not care for it. For many years I mulled making it all over to Clary after Father died. Using the inheritance from my mother that was due to me at age twenty-five, I was going to make a new start elsewhere, away from here and all the trouble. Far away.

"Since he died, I have been thinking a great deal about this. So, you can have it, *Mother,* and to do what you like with. Move all of your Livingstone relatives in here if you like. Marry poor Maria off to a cousin with a head for sheep."

Her hand with the pistol began to shake a little.

"Put that down, Mrs. Bailey, I beg you." Mr. McPherson said, with a tremor in his voice. His brother was pale as death.

"I don't believe you," she said quietly.

"Come, Mrs. Bailey, you are making all of us very nervous." Percy said.

"How do I know you will give me back all my land?"

"Because that is what we are engaged in just now. McPherson here is an estate agent and auctioneer, and here are the papers. We have been going through them." Alexander spoke in a soothing way as if he were trying to convince a child.

Mrs. Bailey still did not believe him.

“Bill,” said Alexander, nodding to the papers on the drawing room table.

McPherson gathered up the papers with nervous fingers and gingerly advanced toward her.

"Put it down. Put the gun down now. It was all for nothing," Alexander said, shaking his head. "You trying to drown me in Thora Tarn, your sending Clarence to murder Mr. Turnbull dressed as me. You would have got the land anyway."

"All for nothing!" she cried out in a great wail. "All for nothing!"

"Who did you engage to try to drown me?"

"Turnbull! Stupid man!"

"Why did you want Turnbull dead?"

"He threatened me."

"So, you sent Clary to Mr. Turnbull disguised as me? It was an almost perfect plan."

"Yes! It would have worked, but for that interfering girl!"

She trembled violently and extended her hand greedily for the papers held by Mr. McPherson.

"Show me, show me!" she ordered.

"Put the gun down first," Alex said firmly. She placed it on the table next to her. At a nod from him, McPherson handed her the papers. She took them greedily in both hands.

Alexander sprung forward with the agility of a cat and took possession of the gun.

"Did we hear an admission of murder?" he said then, looking around.

"Did we hear an admission of attempted murder also?" McPherson asked.

She looked at them, all three, and turned around to look for the gun, but in vain. The McPherson men advanced and held her firmly. Alexander rang the bell to rouse the housekeeper and maid from bed to secure Mrs. Bailey in a room until the police could be sent for in the morning. Mrs. Bailey admitted everything, with a sort of bravado, to the police, and even told them, with pride and regret, about the mushrooms. Alexander had completely forgotten them.

"Would you really have returned the land to us?" Lydia asked as she was being taken away.

"No. Not a chance." Alexander said.

"You wretch!"

McPherson congratulated him for his quick mind. "It was a close-run thing though," he said. "I would not have liked to see her shoot herself."

"I was her target. That was the only thing I could say to distract her, for she's obsessed with getting it back."

CHAPTER 67

PROPOSAL

Tess was concerned to see that Mrs. Bailey's bed had not been slept in. Where was she? She went out to the road, walked a little bit toward Stagtarn Hall, and met Alexander walking toward her in his dark blue greatcoat and muffler.

He told her all, in the middle of the narrow road, with the trees white with frost and the winter morning sending slivers of weak sunlight through the branches.

"She will be going away then," Tess said.

"She may be sentenced to hang, also. Though women often get reprieved. She will most likely go to prison for life."

"What will happen the girls?"

"They will go to her sister Lenore."

Tess was silent.

"What shall I do? Where shall I -? Where do I stand now? What is mine? What isn't?"

"You may do whatever you wish, Tess."

"What I wish is for Mama to return, and that is still so far off. It's too soon to even have heard from her. She may not even know yet that she's free and pardoned. The baby is due in July."

Alexander was silent. He looked up and down the road, as if he did not want to look at her.

“What’s the matter, Alex?” she asked quietly.

“I have to ask you this, Tess. Did you love him? Did you fall in love with him?”

“No.”

“I thought you might have. He led me to believe that you wished to live as man and wife.”

“No, not my wish,” she hung her head, confused, embarrassed, and distressed.

“I’m sorry. It was so indelicate of me to even mention it, but-” He wanted to confess his love there and then, but he did not need to explain. She looked at him suddenly with her clear, almond-shaped dark eyes, illuminated as to the state of his heart.

"You think I loved Clarence! I did not. I feared him. I did my duty. I went to his execution because it was my duty, and he asked me, so piteously. He cried like a baby. He had no friend there but me. He was my husband, and I did this last thing for him. You do not blame me for that?"

Alex remembered the lurid broadsheets. What a fool he had been to allow them to poison his mind!

"No, I do not. It was a fine thing you did."

"I knew that you might not understand it, but I took the chance that you would."

"I understand it. Tess, will you marry me?" He asked her quietly. "You know I love you. I always have loved you."

"But Alex! I love you too, but the baby is Clarence's! How do you feel about the baby?"

"A quarter Livingstone! I can bear it."

"But, will you be able to love it?"

"It will be half-you and yes, I will love him or her as my own."

"I don't want for there to be a situation that existed between you and Clarence. This baby is not your blood. But he will be the eldest and expect to inherit. If you and I have a son, would you not wish for that child to take precedence over Clarence's?"

"I hadn't thought of that," Alex admitted, feeling a fool. Women seemed to see around corners about these matters more than men.

"I'm selling Stagtarn," he told her. "I do not want it. I'm afraid that there's a curse on it or something. As you say, the trouble of this generation could spill over into the next. We will avoid that. Come, let's walk. It's cold." He took her hand. "Did I get a "yes" or a "no" to my proposal?"

"It's an 'I don't know'."

"Do you love me, Tess?"

"You know I do. And it should be simple, but, it isn't."

"Either way, you need protection." He drew her closer. "You are having a child. Will your uncle and aunt look after you?"

"No, for they are going to sell the Arms and retire. I know they won't want me and a wean."

"A wean! You're a Cumberlander."

There was silence as they walked on, their boots making crisp noises on the frosty road.

"Yes," said Tess.

"Yes, you'll marry me?"

"Yes, but after the baby is born, Alex. It would be best."

Tess was still afraid that the baby would make a difference to Alexander. She needed to see that he could love his wicked brother's child.

"If you are uncomfortable where you are, at Beckley House, I can arrange for you to take a house in Carlisle perhaps, with a servant and a nurse. Remember you will have Clarence's money at your disposal soon."

"Perhaps I would like that better than the Livingstone house," she said. "Now, I had better go back to it. Someone has to tell the girls about their mother," she sighed.

"Wait a minute." He drew her close and kissed her. She returned his kiss with warmth and love.

CHAPTER 68

BAD NEWS

Alexander went home a happier man. Stagtarn already looked like a strange house, a house that did not love him, never had, and would be happier to see the back of him, as happy as he would be to see the back of it.

There was not much farm work to be done in winter, and what was to be done, the agent and labourers could manage well, so he was not required. He went that very day to take a house in Carlisle for Tess.

It was not yet time for his big adventure, and he doubted it would happen now. It did not matter. Tess was healthy, and as spring came in, and summer, she suffered not at all and was well taken care of. He visited her once every week.

Mrs. Lydia Bailey was tried and found guilty of the murder of Reginald Turnbull, sentenced to death, and reprieved because she was a woman. The girls went to Aunt Lenore, who lived in Carlisle, so they and Tess saw much of each other.

In July, Tess gave birth to a little girl. She named her Elizabeth Mary after her mother. She was healthy and thrived.

Her mother should be home toward the end of the year! Alex promised that when she arrived at Stagtarn Hall, the only address she had for Tess, that he would take her straight to her side. Stagtarn was not selling as quickly as he hoped, and he was determined that no Livingstone should purchase it via a third party. Such a business may well be afoot. To have such news reaching Mrs. Bailey in prison would spell a great victory for her after all. It must not happen.

"Alex, I should love for Mama to be here at our wedding," Tess said. "Can we wait?"

"Of course, my love. We can wait. There will be double joy!"

But in October, there was a letter. Alexander brought it to her. She was sitting in the garden getting some late autumn sunshine with the baby asleep in her crib.

"Why would she send a letter, when she could be home as soon as it arrived?" Tess wondered, opening it.

Alexander stood about. He nervously toyed with a piece of loose wood on the fence. The pardon had been granted, and Mrs. Woods should be home very soon. But why send a letter in advance? Was there some delay? He turned around to see Tess' head slumped onto her breast, and tears rolling down her cheeks.

The letter lay on her lap. He picked it up.

Dear Tess, how happy I am to have a pardon, how great it is that the crime was solved. I will not waste words on the culprits.

Aunt Belle wrote to tell me you are married! If you wrote to tell me, I have not got that letter yet. But since you're Roman Catholic, did you get permission from the bishop to marry a Protestant? If not, you must go and get permission or you are living in sin, Miss Tess.

Tess, you must be very brave when I tell you that I have made my life here and have got married. I am not coming back to England. His name is Sean Delaney and he's the son of an Irish convict who was sent here for stealing a sheep. We love each other very much and get on like a house on fire. Another Catholic! I seem to be attracted to them. He is writing this letter for me, and he sends love.

No doubt you're disappointed I am not coming back. Bear up, love. Maybe you will come out here if Clarence is willing to? Tell him it's a great young country and farmers are very welcome, there are sheep farms springing up everywhere. All my Love, your mother and stepfather Sean.

"Oh Tess, Tess." He dropped to his knees and drew her head upon his breast. She sobbed.

"I was so looking forward - but how can I even think of going - look, I'm not even married, it seems! What does that make my little Elizabeth? Oh, I'm so confused I don't know what is what anymore. Will I go? Will I not go? What's going to happen? Oh, my goodness! That money I inherited from Clarence isn't mine after all! Or is it?"

"We'll both go to Australia," Alexander said, taking her hands in his and rubbing them with eagerness. "We'll both go. Will we? Will we go and join your mother?"

As he thought about the possibility, his face lit up with the prospect of getting away, the sea voyage and starting over in a new country. He was going on his big adventure! The adventure he had dreamed of when he was a little sickly lad confined to his bed in the nursery. And the woman he loved would be by his side. Would they do it?

"And no inheritance problems either," he added, placing his hand on little Elizabeth's head. "I'll adopt her. Stagtarn will be gone. We'll leave everything Livingstone after us. She will be a Bailey, and I promise to do fair by her, Tess. She's a bonny little girl. Gretna Green is just up the road. Will we run up there tomorrow?"

"I have to get permission from my bishop, you silly man!" Tess flung herself into his arms. "Didn't you read what my mother wrote?"

"Where is he?" Alex asked plaintively. "And will we go to Australia?"

"Well, I shall go! Eliza and me! Are you joining us?" Tess could hardly contain her excitement.

They found Bishop Hanly the next day. He was rather upset that Tess had never had instruction in her faith, and she promised him she would get it in Australia. He gave his permission, and three days later he married them.

Alex never spent another night at Stagtarn Hall.

CHAPTER 69

THE CHRISTMAS BUSH

FIVE YEARS LATER

The little community nestled near the town of Wodonga was growing, and Alexander and Tess had at last finished their new farmhouse. It was a long, low, timber-framed bungalow with large, airy rooms located only three miles from the main road from Sydney to Melbourne, both established towns by now. The outside was painted a cool white and blue, for though it was built in the shadiest part of a hill, it was still hot. A stone chimney piece rose at one end. The outside verandah faced west overlooking a lake. Alexander could not live without seeing a cool body of water every day. Beyond that, gently rolling hills looked a misty bluish-green from afar. The Snowy Mountains. Wattles and willow myrtle trees outside the verandah gave shade. There was a lawn, if a patch of scrub could be called that, and a few sheep were always to be found grazing there. A pathway of red sand led to the gate, and a row of native flowers, blooms they had never seen or heard of before, but no less beautiful than English ones, grew near the fence. The queen of them all was a thick bush given to them as a gift. It was rather dull for the whole year, but around December burst into bright red blooms as if bred for festivities, so it was named the Christmas Bush.

The Baileys had seen new animals and colourful birds, and they were still discovering marvels about this strange place on the other side of the world from England. This land was still full of wonder to the emigrants, though their children would regard their surroundings as commonplace.

Behind the house, extending for a distance, were the stables, outbuildings, and the stockmen's quarters. It got a little rowdy there sometimes, but with bushrangers around with their covetous eyes on the horses and livestock, it was good to have protection. The scrub behind the huts stretched miles and miles away, off to the vast untamed outback.

The interior was simple but comfortable. A few paintings from England and Scotland hung on the walls.

Today was Christmas Eve. Tess perspired as she took a pot out of the oven. She raised her head when she heard at last the creak of the gate and a wagon trundle over the rough pathway, getting louder with every foot. She knew her children were watching excitedly from the veranda steps, for Grandmama and Grandpapa were coming to visit.

"They're here!" she cried to Alexander out the back window where he was clearing some unsightly brush from the yard before his in-laws came. He had been meaning to do it for weeks now, and only this morning Tess had given him a very mild reproach about it.

He loved his life in this Great South Land., He loved his family and was loved in return. He had to own that it was an adventure of very hard work; Australia wasn't giving up the fruits of the land without mighty effort. But he and Tess were luckier than most settlers. They came with money. They bought their land outright, unlike the bounty migrants who had to work it and pay rent to the government until they could claim it as their own.

He never thought about the Livingstones. He had largely forgotten that Eliza was not his. He thought her the most affectionate, cheerful child in the world, and she adored him. She thought he was her father. Lily wanted to come out to them to live. She felt isolated and unhappy among the Baileys. It had emerged during the trial that she was Mr. Turnbull's daughter. They would welcome her, and she'd be company every day for Tess.

"Grandmama! Grandpapa!" The little children rushed out to surround the wagon and to greet the smiling middle-aged woman who swept them up in her arms one by one. Eliza had been joined by Ephraim and Michael, who was barely two.

"Merry Christmas!" Tess' mother came into the house and embraced her daughter. “My, how big those children are since July! It’s good to see you, Tess. I love the house colour.” She chattered on. “Such a large house, Tess. I’m happy for you.”

The Delaneys had not much means. They were ‘selectors’, who had to earn their land. It pleased Tess to be able to help her mother, and Alexander was good to them.

Delaney, or Grandpapa, was unloading the wagon and bringing in gaily wrapped presents and bottles of lemonade. Alex had halted his brush-clearing and came around to help him. His father-in-law had given him good advice and practical help in learning how to farm this stubborn parched earth so different from the lush English countryside, for they grew their own food.

“You have come laden with presents. It’s too much,” Tess gave another mild reproach, to her mother this time.

"I love Christmas! Is it Christmas yet?" asked Ephraim, who was wild with excitement.

"I love it too!" cried Michael.

"And me!" Lizzie said.

"And me," Tess said. "Except for all the work, of course! What a gift children are, Mama. They've taught me to love Christmas again."

"Fancy a cold beer?" Alexander asked Sean. Alex had grown very tanned and muscular from the hard work, and he was rapidly becoming Australian in every way.

"Cold? How could it be cold?"

"I got ice from Sydney," Alex said, opening a chest by the wall to reveal large chunks of rapidly-melting ice inside with all kinds of food and drink stacked inside.

"Well, I never! Ice in summer! Elizabeth, come 'ere, see this."

"The beer was the first thing he put in there," Tess chuckled.

"Can I have beer, too?" Ephraim said.

"No, but you can come out on the verandah and drink your lemonade with us," his father said, and the little boy was satisfied.

"Any news?" Alex asked Sean as they went outside.

"Well, the bushrangers…there could be a big blow-up one of these days." The Delaneys lived at Glenrowan, near some wild families who were constantly at loggerheads with the police.

The women settled down to chat.

"I remember when you first heard of Christmas you were all excited about it. It was a summer day in Preston, " Mrs. Delaney said.

Tess went to the dresser and took the leather-bound missal that had belonged to her father from the top shelf.

"I still have the petals," she said. "They're a little worse for wear by now. But I have been telling Eliza the story of the rose petals, and she is enchanted. I have to tell it to her over and over."

"Oh, Tess, what a journey we have made, you and me!" her mother said as Eliza climbed onto her lap and snuggled into her. "Happiness, loss, despair, hope...but we have a lot to thank God for. Is Alex happy here?" she asked in a hushed tone. "He's not the rich gentleman he was at 'ome!"

"He's happy and says he wouldn't change a thing. He has a swim every day, rain or shine, and I became very agitated when I heard of crocodiles, but he says there aren't any in the lake. We're happy, Mama. This life has its challenges, but we're committed to it. Hard work." She swung the baby Michael on to her lap and gave him a biscuit. "I wouldn't swop anything."

"When I think over our life at Preston, after your father died, I was hard on you, Tess. But I always had great love for you. You know that. I thought about you all the time. On the prison ship out, the thought of being reunited with you someday kept me goin'. And all the time during my first days, months, and years 'ere, worryin' about you and wonderin' if you missed me as much as I missed you."

"I did, Mama. I missed you all the time. But Aunt Belle wrote bad things about me."

"Oh, Belle! I shouldn't have paid any attention. It was very hard, tryin' to be a mother from so far away. It was impossible."

"You gave me good advice about the man I should choose. A sober, generous, and even-tempered man. Alex is all that! Cup of tea, Mama?"

"Oh yes, of course. It's never too hot for tea, Tess. You are looking well, child."

Mrs. Delaney knew the entire story of what had happened to Tess. She was very grateful to Alexander and firmly believed that God had sent him to her daughter. Yes, she was a woman of faith now. Faith was very important to the whole family.

And they all loved Christmas, even Tess, as she explained to the ever-curious Eliza what 'Boughs of Holly' were and why the carol said to 'Deck the Halls' with them. It was all to celebrate the birth of Jesus, our Saviour. The joy that He was born to us, and He came to love us and to save us from our sins.

Later on, they would hitch the wagon and go down in the cool of the night to Midnight Mass. Tomorrow they'd feast.

~

THANK YOU FOR CHOOSING A PUREREAD BOOK!

We hope you enjoyed the story, and as a way to thank you for choosing PureRead we'd like to send you this free book, and other fun reader rewards…

Click here for your free copy of Whitechapel Waif
PureRead.com/victorian

Thanks again for reading.
See you soon!

LOVE VICTORIAN ROMANCE?

If you enjoyed this story why not continue straight away with other books in our PureRead Victorian Romance library?

Read them all...

Victorian Slum Girl's Dream

Poor Girl's Hope

The Lost Orphan of Cheapside

Born a Workhouse Baby

The Lowly Maid's Triumph

Poor Girl's Hope

The Victorian Millhouse Sisters

Dora's Workhouse Child

Saltwick River Orphan

Workhouse Girl and The Veiled Lady

OUR GIFT TO YOU

AS A WAY TO SAY THANK YOU WE WOULD LOVE TO SEND YOU THIS BEAUTIFUL STORY FREE OF CHARGE.

Click here for your free copy of Whitechapel Waif

PureRead.com/victorian

Printed in Great Britain
by Amazon

10078395R00185